ELECTRA
My life in a world of violence and bloodshed

I0554591

Jeffrey Peter Clarke

ELECTRA
My life in a world of
violence and bloodshed

FICTION4ALL

Locations mentioned in this novel

Prologue

What might the grey, part tumbled Cyclopean stones of Mycenae, a city said once to be rich in gold, tell us of her past if they could speak? The great wall surrounding the city, standing proud to keep out her enemies some three and a half thousand years ago, today proclaims in silence the depredations of men and of time. Through her famed Lion Gate, above which the rampant beasts of carved stone remain standing, once passed worthies, emissaries and traders from the Peloponnese and much of Greece beyond. Her alleyways, her squares, then alive with calls and chatter, with careering, pestering children and yapping dogs, offer now only gaping emptiness to birds wheeling darkly in the sky above.

The palace, once looking down upon the city, once a centre of power and wealth, of vibrant columns, richly frescoed walls, proudly displayed bronze armour, weapons and trophies, lies open and desolate. Long forgotten are the finely attired courtiers who spiced the air with talk and laughter. It was here the bard played and sang of great deeds, here beyond memory the rulers and their coterie gathered and contrived the fate of others.

The gods of old are gone but could those walls speak through the sighing breezes of night they would surely have dark tales to tell; tales of deceit, of intrigue and of murder. They might even now weep blood.

Chapter 1
The Voice of Electra

That I, Electra, a daughter of the one-time great and victorious Agamemnon, King of Mycenae, hero of the Trojan war, am here to speak as I do is a blessing bestowed by the gods who have seen fit to preserve me until this day in a world of dark and devious scheming. To understand why my life has taken the path it has means your knowing the history of my family, of events that took place well before I was born, of what I have witnessed and what I have been a part of through my tender years and beyond. Somewhat involved, I have to say, but I must here occupy myself in relating it, though this bizarre tide of events will manifest itself also through the voices of others.

I sit by the window in the comfort of what is now my occasional retreat from the busy court below. These modest rooms used to be my living area and were for long my prison. They are located above the palace which rises above all other buildings at the south of the town, its parapets lined with those stylised, stone bulls' horns common throughout the larger cities of Greece and those of her islands. Within the palace is the great hall, what we refer to as the megaron, the social heart of the palace where the court is held. Here stands the royal throne – the throne from where, long ago, Agamemnon ruled. The palace is quite out of keeping with the rugged stone and timber buildings that occupy most of Mycenae though all are designed to resist those occasional earthquakes from which our land suffers. For the palace of Mycenae, as with those of many other cities throughout Greece, an attempt has been made to emulate the style if not the grandeur of the great and famous palace of Knossos on Crete; witnessed by some but little more than hearsay to others. Should you be familiar with Knossos then you surely will know what I mean.

Anyone visiting the ruler of Mycenae would enter via a flagstoned portico whose great stone lintel is supported by a pair of russet coloured, downward tapering columns. On passing through a frescoed anteroom they first would be confronted by the large, ceremonial circular hearth where much of the day burns a lively fire from which smoke rises to small windows above. The hearth is flanked by four great columns, these colourfully painted and rising to a profusely decorated, coffered ceiling. A few steps beyond this hearth rests the royal throne of scalloped-edge, alabaster, draped with lavish coverings and a soft cushion for the comfort of its occupant. A few steps from the throne, seated by a column as I well recall, was once to be found pale-gowned, white-bearded old Leucon. There he played his lyre and recited the deeds of heroes. His fund of heroes was considerable and their deeds grew ever more impressive with the passing years. Displayed about the walls are the weapons of violence, swords, spears and axes of gleaming bronze. There, too, the heavy, man-covering, figure-of-eight shields and their smaller, lighter companions better suited in close combat for the forward, brutal push. Portrayed about the flat, plastered walls between these clusters of objects are colourfully painted armed warriors frozen in prancing postures of aggression.

The modest walls of my incense-laden retreat are brightly painted with images more pleasing to my eye; swooping birds and the wild creatures of nature. In a room next to this there stands that greatest of luxuries in Mycenae, a private bath with hot water dispensed from a valve set into the wall. Yes, hot water. There is an odd-smelling soap made from the fat of slaughtered animals, this cooked together with wood ashes, but it serves its purpose well enough. The water is drawn from an adjacent chamber, not accessible from my bathroom, by braziers heating a tank that also feeds two other sets of rooms similar to my own, these once occupied by others we are soon to meet. Close to me a polished bronze mirror stands upon an elegantly carved wooden table together with my gold and silver inlaid ivory comb and my perfumed oils in small, decorated pots. There, too lie the jewelled and bodily adornments of gold and even more precious silver, these of a kind so valued by others but, I often feel, of lesser worth to me. Further back stands the loom, now sad and abandoned. This I made much use of when held here against my will.

I gaze into the mirror. I see long hair, hair the colour of ripening corn, cascade freely about my white-gowned shoulders. My blue eyes are bright, my cheeks unblemished. I offer the mirror a smile, just a little smile, and I think upon what has been

11

and what might have been of my life. A warm, gentle breeze touches my cheek. My fingers embrace a gilded goblet and I drink honeyed wine poured for me from an amphora by Melia, a young woman, once a slave of the palace, now my personal attendant. Yes, she is dedicated to my worldly pleasures when, after my bath, she caresses my body with those perfumed oils and so delicately massages my flesh. Oh, what a comfort she is, and was in this blighted city when most of our best men were gone to fight at Troy. Yes, Troy. Memories of Troy, a theatre of heroism and death, will echo through ages beyond our imagination. Perhaps what happened there will change the whole world.

I look out now beyond the mighty cyclopean wall that circles all about to protect our city from invasion, though as you will learn, that same wall has served also to contain many evils. I peer down to the land below where olive groves and orchards bask in the clear morning light of a newly risen sun. I see where cattle, pigs and sheep are gathered together or are free to roam, and further still I gaze to where woodlands and farms spread way into the hilly distance. All is peaceful now throughout the Peloponnese though conflict has never seemed far away. These have been violent times throughout much of Greece and beyond but nowhere has it been more manifest than here at Mycenae in what people refer to still as the House of Atreus; a house cursed by the gods. And because Atreus once ruled this city as a powerful king it is his afflicted tale I must first relate for that curse was to be handed down through generations. I ask now for your patience.

In their earlier days Atreus and his brother Thyestes were nobles of Elis, a town in the north-west Peloponnese. They fled from their city with a small number of followers after murdering their half-brother in a family squabble. By all accounts Atreus was a big man, course in manner, long-bearded and aggressive, whereas his brother, inclined more to the refined life of the court, was less assertive. Thyestes three legitimate sons also joined their father so as to avoid the vengeance of others of that town falling upon them, though his wife chose to remain there, as did those sons of his by a woman of the court. It is related how, some time before the murder, an oracle within one of Elis' temples had prophesied one of the brothers would become king. King of where, and which of them it might be was never made clear, though at the time it seemed to them of scant importance. But then oracles are oracles; if they prove true they are usually remembered and when they do not they are easily forgotten.

The brothers travelled eastward to Mycenae, then at war with Athens. There, finding her king, Eurystheus, and his only son had recently been killed in battle and the court in turmoil, Atreus, on recalling the words of the Elian oracle, seized the throne of Mycenae. Thyestes, never given an opportunity to discuss the matter with his brother, was incensed and claimed the throne ought to have been his through his greater familiarity with court affairs. The bombastic Atreus, his position quickly assured, was not inclined to argue over this so, for the time being, the resentful Thyestes occupied

13

himself in hunting and the pleasures of the court. Pleasures of the Mycenaean court being mainly its wine and its women who dressed then, as now, in the commonly followed Cretan palace fashion of long, flounced and colourful dresses with short-sleeved bodices that left their breasts exposed. Also in the Cretan style, real or imagined, they wore diadems and beads twisted in their hair, bracelets, necklaces, precious rings and on occasion, large gold or silver hooped earrings. Yes, many of the great cities of Greece vied to affect the image of Knossos.

Now established as king of a wealthy and powerful city, Atreus married Airope, a renowned beauty and daughter of the dead Eurystheus, an act that would help secure his position as ruler. By her he had two sons; firstly Agamemnon, a year later Menelaus, then a girl who did not for long survive. All might have been well for Atreus and for Mycenae except that Airope, more a free spirit than Atreus would have wished, had all along preferred the more refined company of Thyestes. This she enjoyed in full on those occasions when the king himself was out hunting. Through this torrid relationship Thyestes perceived a means of getting back at his brother, though how this was to be achieved in the long run could not have been clear to him at the time.

Atreus became increasingly suspicious of his brother's reluctance to accompany him when away from the city and decided, as Thyestes was reluctant to account for his activities, he must be busy plotting mischief within the palace. A bid, perhaps, for the throne. Consequently, Atreus ordered him banished from Mycenae together with his sons.

Thyestes' affair with Airope however, had been impossible to keep secret. All the court, aware of what had been going on, gossiped as people are prone to do, but dared say nothing to the king. And, yes, as you may have guessed, Atreus, though last to know, did hear of it shortly after his brother's departure; informed by one of his female attendants who Thyestes had abused and insulted when drunk. Atreus, on realising he'd been made a fool of throughout palace and perhaps all the city, was possessed by a vengeful rage that, helped by surfeit of wine, turned his mind away from reason. He ordered members of the palace guard to conduct a protesting Airope out of the city and to the coast where it was rumoured she was thrown into the sea and drowned. That same day he appointed an envoy to set off and locate Thyestes with a message of forgiveness, of reconciliation and assurance that he would be welcomed back to Mycenae and appointed joint ruler as should have been the case all along.

The envoy returned, accompanied by Thyestes with his three sons. All were warmly greeted by Atreus who declared a banquet would be held for Thyestes the following day. Sensing deceit and wary of his brother's motives, Thyestes insisted his sons go to and remain in the temple of Zeus where their safety, as custom demanded, would be assured. Atreus, however, was of no mind to observe customs. The promised banquet was held next evening in the megaron. It was a lavish affair by all accounts with entertainers, singing and wine in abundance. I'm told what then happened by one of the male court attendants who was witness there, one now an aged acolyte at our temple of Zeus.

When the dining and entertainment was ended, Atreus called in two of the palace guards who laid upon the table before Thyestes a number of personal items lately possessed by his three sons, including the daggers each had worn at his belt. He then informed Thyestes that the boys had been executed and that the meat their father had just eaten was not that of a sheep but the flesh, specially prepared and cooked for him, from one of his son's severed limbs. Thyestes, believing in full what he'd been told, leaped from the table to flee in stark horror from the megaron and into the night before anyone could stop him.

Since hearing this I have wondered often to what depths some men will stoop when blinded by vengeance. It was later learned Thyestes had somehow avoided capture and made his way to Sicyon, a coastal town to the north of Mycenae and somewhat closer to Corinth. There he entered the temple of Apollo, one renowned for punishing the wicked, there sacrificed to the god and laid the curse upon Atreus and all of Mycenae for what her king, his own brother, had done. Apollo, evidently, was listening and was sympathetic, and so too was mighty Zeus. Perhaps for a time Atreus was satisfied with the appalling act he had committed but his contentment was destined not to last and others, too, would suffer because of it.

Also in Sicyon, quite by chance, for surely the gods would not have planned it, was a daughter of

Thyestes. She had, when still a child, been sent there by her mother to avoid the family troubles in Elis and, now a young woman, she served at the temple of Athena.

It is said what had happened at Mycenae had afflicted Thyestes' mind and driven him to consume an excess of wine, something he was anyway not adverse to. Having squandered much of one day at an inn, he wandered after dark into the temple of Athena where, in a drunken act of lust, he attacked Pelopia as she made sacrifice at the altar and raped her without knowing or caring who she was. He had thrown aside his sword while there and having forgotten to retrieve it, was unable when awakening next day to recall where he'd been and all but nothing of the vile act that he'd committed. Pelopia did of course recognise the sword as that belonging to her attacker and was tempted through an onset of shame to fall upon it and end her own life. She did not, but decided in future to ensure the company of one or more of those serving at the temple when not in her private rooms. There was no one she felt she could turn to and disclose what had happened – not even grey-bearded Thesprotus, the aging king of Sicyon who, though treating Pelopia very much as his own daughter was, so most people considered, somewhat ineffectual as a ruler.

Within a month of Thyestes' fleeing Mycenae his curse in the form of a pestilence had descended upon the city. Thought by many to be the onset of plague, it was feared this would soon affect the entire population within and without the city wall. The priests of Zeus' temple were quick to point out that this was indeed punishment for the murder of Thyestes three sons at the very altar of their god and only an appropriate sacrifice would counter the affliction. Sacrifice at the altar of Zeus is what Atreus undertook in person; not simply goats or pigs but three young male slaves falsely accused of offenses; one for each of the murdered youths. After this sanctified butchering he also offered a number of gold vessels and to his amazement as well as to that of the priests, the pestilence, if indeed that's what it was, receded almost as quickly as it had taken hold.

On consulting one of the priests who claimed oracular powers, Atreus was advised to seek out his brother and return him to Mycenae. Atreus, it was said, concluded that this could mean dead or alive and set out at once to Sicyon with an armed party. With them were gifts for the king, Thesprotus, as custom required, for Sicyon was at the time on reasonably good terms with Mycenae. Thyestes, however, on hearing of his dear brother's arrival with armed men, had understandably taken refuge some distance away from the town.

It was when in discussion with Thesprotus that Atreus spotted Pelopia with her female companions. Like the women of Thesprotus' court who dressed in the Cretan manner, by which I mean with their breasts revealed, Pelopia, a woman of great beauty, was likewise attired in keeping with her priestly status. She struck Atreus as most desirable and the king, in noting his attention, seems to have conceived certain possibilities. Thesprotus had doubtless conducted formalities with Atreus when he ordered wine to be brought and summoned Pelopia to join them. As Pelopia had never been to Mycenae she had only distant memories of Atreus, her uncle. The now deceptively calm-faced and on this occasion well behaved Atreus she found most appealing in spite of his less than cultivated appearance, his table manners, and his greater age. I'm sure you will agree, there is at times no accounting for female taste. Thesprotus, so it is told, noted her attraction, introduced her as his daughter and had Atreus thinking the King of Sicyon meant his true rather than his make-believe daughter. Pelopia said nothing to cast doubt upon this casual deception and so it was maintained.

Atreus stayed at Sicyon for many days during which he spent much time with Pelopia, encouraged all along by her assumed father who entertained them together as often as possible. Thesprotus may have been somewhat ineffectual as a ruler but in desiring to maintain his alliance with Mycenae he was anxious to see a bond develop between the two. Had Pelopia known of Atreus' past deeds and in particular the fate of Airope, things would have been very different but soon enough he asked Thesprotus for her hand in marriage. With this the king was eager to agree and offered arrangements for the ceremony there at Sicyon. Apart from his acquiring a beautiful wife, Atreus saw this marriage as maintaining Sicyon as a dependent ally after Thesprotus' death. Pelopia feared Thyestes might return after Atreus' departure and dreaded encountering this otherwise unknown man who had so brutally defiled her. The court of Mycenae, so she imagined, ought to be a better proposition. Such are the misconceptions people may at times have.

After the wedding, a relatively quiet affair, arrangements for Pelopia to transfer to Mycenae with her attendant girls and her possessions were undertaken but by this time Pelopia had discovered she was pregnant and realised it would soon be impossible to conceal the fact. Atreus decided no more time should be wasted before returning to Mycenae in case it was to there Thyestes had gone, hoping to take advantage of his brother's absence. Pelopia begged for more time to have her affairs put into order before she would be escorted from Sicyon to take her place by his side and to this Atreus, with a rare show of condescension, agreed.

After his departure Pelopia retired to the privacy of the rooms allocated to her at the palace by Thesprotus where she was visited only by her most trusted attendants. Messengers eventually arrived from Mycenae wanting to know when she was to leave Sicyon and join her new husband. They were told she had much yet to attend to because of her position as priestess at Athena's temple but would shortly set out to join the increasingly impatient Atreus. When the child was born an envoy was sent to Mycenae to inform Atreus that Pelopia was at last on her way to him. Pelopia's male child, together with his father's, *her* father's sword, accompanied the party when early one morning they set off to Mycenae, hidden from view inside a covered wagon.

Later that day, with the city in sight, they stopped a while. Pelopia's plans for the child were not to include his arrival at Mycenae. Her feelings were much in conflict over the one to whom she had given birth but she nevertheless determined to abandon him to whatever fate might offer. With those who accompanied her sworn to silence, Pelopia alone took the child, together with the sword abandoned by Thyestes at Athena's temple, and laid him out of sight, bundled in warm clothing, on a gentle hillside slope. I can only imagine her feelings; fraught with regret at leaving him to die, possibly crushed mercilessly in the jaws of some wild beast, yet unable herself to face the prospect of seeing him thrive and achieve manhood before an unsympathetic Atreus.

Pelopia's arrival at Mycenae gave rise to celebrations presided over by the king, with food and wine in most generous quantities. She was that day appointed her own slaves while her personal attendants from Sicyon were permitted also to remain with her. They would keep their secret in spite of what was soon to happen, yes, for as long as Pelopia lived.

Agamemnon and Menelaus, the infant children of Atreus and the recently disposed of Airope, took to Pelopia at once and she to them. Did Pelopia ever inquire about their true mother? That I do not know but I cannot believe her ear was not in time touched by rumour.

But then the unexpected. A shepherd had come upon the abandoned child and had taken him home. Unsure what to do, he and his wife had kept and fed the tiny boy for several days until deciding they could no longer manage. They brought him, together with the sword, into the market place of Mycenae where they set about with reward in mind to inquire if anyone knew to whom he belonged. It chanced that day Pelopia herself had entered the market and on approaching a group of onlookers, saw there her own child. Perhaps this was what the gods intended for she was unable to ignore or to reject him a second time and returned to the palace taking him with her. There she presented him to Atreus and suggested that, because of the finely crafted sword, which the king might have recognised had he examined it more closely, the child must have belonged to someone of high status and so ought to be taken care of; this in case he'd been abducted and therefore would be much sought after. It seems Atreus was in a benevolent mood because he accepted Pelopia's suggestion that they retain the boy. I wonder if he didn't instinctively see in the child features of his own family. He agreed, if no one claimed him, that they might bring him up as a serving companion to the older Agamemnon and Menelaus. After a month, when no one had come forward to claim the boy, they decided his name would be Aegisthus.

There now followed an unusual period of peace throughout much of the Peloponnese during which time Atreus renewed a treaty with nearby Argos concluded years before by his predecessor, Eurystheus. But more importantly he secured an alliance with Tyndareus, King of Sparta, a powerful city which lay to the south of Mycenae. Each ruler was welcomed by the other on official as well as casual visits and they would often set out hunting together.

Aegisthus was approaching early manhood but because of his lesser importance at the court of Mycenae it's told how he had grown jealous of Atreus' true sons and harboured a deep-seated resentment toward them and their father. Atreus in turn had come to regret his adoption of Aegisthus because the boy had by all accounts developed a manner of arrogance and insolence. It's said to have caused Pelopia much distress in trying to mollify the easily angered Atreus over this.

Through the following years however, rumours had persisted that Thyestes, Aegisthus' unknowing father, having returned to Sicyon, was heard boasting how he would dispose of Atreus by assassination if he was unable to raise an armed force. Atreus ascribed these rumours to his brother's love of strong wine but nevertheless found them a source of much irritation and considered enough was enough. By now his sons, Agamomnon and Menelaus, had reached manhood. As a test of their courage and bargaining abilities Atreus sent them off to locate Thyestes and persuade him to return to Mycenae. Should he do so, ran the promise, then past disputes might be set aside and the kingship of Mycenae shared equally between the two brothers. Thyestes was to be assured as well that his three sons were never killed but sent into exile and might be summoned back to join him. We may think Atreus naive in expecting his brother to believe a word of it, but no; should Thyestes refuse the king's offer then they were to kill him and return to Mycenae with his severed head in a basket.

On their arrival at Sicyon, however, Agamemnon and Menelaus found Thyestes had departed the town some months before. They learned as well that he had stayed in one of the inns where, his mouth loosened by wine, he had freely informed others how he would return in disguise to Mycenae and deal fatally with his brother. When hearing this, Atreus was livid and concluded that Thyestes might already be in the city or even somewhere in the palace which, if so, meant his own life was now in danger. On his questioning the palace staff and slaves it appeared a furtive, cowl-headed stranger *had* been spotted in an older, rarely frequented part of the palace used mainly for storage, and on occasion even begging for left-over food at the kitchens, a not uncommon practice. A kitchen overseer, having noticed such a man, described having glimpsed an elaborate sword at his side. The description given, though somewhat vague, was close enough to that of Thyestes to have Atreus send out a slave boy to ascertain the intruder's exact location at night. The boy had remained hidden over several nights and reported seeing the stranger enter a particular room on numerous occasions.

It was to Aegisthus, now a strapping youth, the king turned to have his family problems addressed together with promises of enhanced status should he succeed. It seems Atreus had no wish to let Agamemnon or Menelaus, his own flesh and blood, risk mortal danger and hoped Aegisthus and

Thyestes would kill each other. It's the way matters were dealt with in this happy household.

Some about the palace are still ready and willing to relate what happened in detail all those years ago. They tell how Aegisthus found his way into the room where the intruder was sleeping and of how Thyestes woke up and managed to seize his own sword. There must have been enough light in there since, before either man managed to strike a blow against the other, each recognised the sword the other was intending to use as being from the same workshop, almost identical in style and ornamentation. In the shadowed secrecy of that room they set aside their weapons and each revealed to the other his own identity. Yes, they were father and son and what an amazing revelation that must have been. Both now had a strong grudge against Atreus so instead of Aegisthus killing his newly discovered true father, Thyestes prevailed upon his newfound son to murder Atreus instead and it would seem Aegisthus didn't need much persuading. Later, after darkness had fallen, he went up to the king's chamber, ordered away the two slaves guarding its entrance, strode inside and finding Atreus alone, cleaved his skull with one blow of the very sword that was earlier intended to slay Thyestes.

Now was Thyestes' chance to seize the throne he claimed was his all along but he did nothing until Pelopia discovered her husband's murdered body in its blood-soaked bed. Thyestes appeared before her, pretended shocked surprise as he had so wished for reconciliation with his brother. With her permission, for Pelopia was too confused over this novel co-incidence to do otherwise, he commandeered the palace guard and, with her by his side to confirm his authority, ordered an investigation to find who had committed the deed. He needed to identify someone for his brother's death, naturally, and decided it had to be Atreus' personal slaves found earlier guarding his private chamber. The wretched men were tortured into confessing the deed by means of hot brands applied to their flesh, then duly executed. But worse was to come.

Thyestes summoned grief-stricken Pelopia to the private chamber where Aegisthus waited. There Aegisthus handed her his sword, the one with which she was of course familiar, and revealed to her that it had been left behind in Athena's temple at Sicyon that fateful day by the very man who now stood by his side. Her own father! By all accounts she was horror-stricken and, with neither man caring to prevent it, she turned the blade about and fell upon it, so ending a life too dreadful to bear. To that loathsome pair who witnessed the act her life meant nothing.

With Thyestes now taking the throne of Mycenae and in collusion with Aegisthus as his planned successor, Agamemnon and Menelaus, though fit young men and fully trained in arms, well knew, as sons of Atreus, they faced certain death if they remained in the city. Thyestes would, as the brother of Atreus, demand total allegiance of the palace guard who he intended he would use to eliminate any opposition. Agamemnon and Menelaus took whatever possessions they were able to carry, left Mycenae before Thyestes was able to act against them and eventually made their way to Sparta where they were offered the protection of her king, Tyndareus. Tyndareus was shocked upon learning of Atreus' death; the death of one who he had regarded as a most convenient ally.

But now I must relate what was told of Tyndareus' own circumstances. This powerful ruler and his wife, Leda, had two sons who had left Sparta to pursue adventures of their own in the wider world east of the Peloponnese and the king had heard nothing more of them. Tyndareus' two other children were both fair-haired girls, Clytemnestra and Helen, each wayward in her behaviour and each a year or so younger than Agamemnon and Menelaus. The alluring Clytemnestra was already promised to Tantalus, King of Pisa, a town to the west of the Peloponnese, though it's said she was far from happy over this arrangement. Her younger sister, Helen was not as yet allocated to any in marriage though it was claimed she was quite irresistible to men and had many suitors begging for her hand. Yes, the two girls were considered great beauties and it's said they took full advantage of this.

Tyndareus, in accepting the two refugees from Mycenae into his court, saw much advantage in regarding them as his own sons. Soon enough they were dining regularly with Tyndareus' in his private chambers and were setting out on the hunt with him during the day. Prior to her departing for Pisa, dark-haired, forceful Agamemnon had developed a burning desire for Clytemnestra and that yearning

27

was to persist for long afterwards with dire results. The lithe, copper-haired, more discreet Menelaus in turn was stricken with the seductive Helen and Tyndareus perceived a great opportunity in this. He offered Menelaus adoption and role as his successor in Sparta with marriage to Helen as a means of consolidating his position, saying that as his true sons, even if still alive, had deserted the kingdom, they no longer had claim to his throne. This Menelaus accepted with great enthusiasm. To Agamemnon, Tyndareus offered armed assistance in the taking of his rightful throne at Mycenae with renewal of their alliance. This was exactly what Agamemnon wanted and within a month arrangements were being made throughout Sparta for both events. The marriage between Helen and Menelaus was by all accounts a grand affair and after this Tyndareus began to gather his forces for the attack upon Mycenae with Agamemnon as his captain.

They set off northwards with over five hundred men, their wagons and supplies. It would be a day's journey so Agamemnon, fully in charge, had determined his warriors would camp unseen in the night some way from Mycenae then attack at first light to catch Thyestes off his guard. Armed men, disguised as traders, had already set off in darkness, circling around the city wall to the north side where lay the renowned Lion Gate with its great oak doors. This they would seize, hold and defend until the main party arrived for the doors were closed only when a threat was anticipated. Its defence was unnecessary however, because those armed men already posted there, on finding out Agamemnon was leader of the intruders, proved willing to change their allegiance. And so did most others when word spread about the city. The palace guard at Mycenae had little respect for Thyestes, especially after rumours of Pelopia's death had begun to circulate and for Aegisthus they held hardly more than contempt. Thyestes, on realising his position was hopeless, quit the throne and, attired in a plain robe, presented himself in submission to Agamemnon. By this time Aegisthus had already fled the city via a postern gate with ample gold and other valuables to whereabouts unknown. The Spartan warriors, therefore, could return home.

You may by now have sensed the atmosphere that pervaded throughout the halls of Mycenae. People must have wondered what Agamemnon would do with Thyestes for mercy was not just then on the newly appointed king's mind. Killing Atreus' wayward brother openly, however, after his peaceful act of surrender, might create a bad impression with his new subjects but this in the end did not to concern him. The following night, Thyestes was seized by some of the guards, taken from the cell where he had spent that day and dragged up to the city wall from where he was hurled to his death in the valley below. Word was put about that Thyestes had attempted to escape and leapt in desperation from the wall. A most convenient solution, don't you think.

Once established on the throne of Atreus with the support of the palace guard and men of the city, not much time would pass before Agamemnon confirmed to the world what a ruthless and aggressive man he really was. Later that same year traders crossing the Peloponnese from Elis, the town from which, you will recall, Atreus and Thyestes originated, were attacked and robbed of their goods at night on their way to Mycenae, with one of them dying from his wounds. The bandits who attacked them, so they asserted, were men of Pisa and they described in detail the goods that had been seized from them. It is told how Agamemnon sent an envoy to present his demands for reparations from Pisa but the man returned four days later with a message from their king, Tantalus, to say that no reparations would be made as he was not responsible for brigands who may or may not have originated from his city. The envoy, however, claimed to have witnessed these same stolen goods being traded in the market square of Pisa.

Tantalus' rash response was good news for Agamemnon and he lost no time in raising men, arms and supplies to attack the Pisans whose town, he surely knew, was smaller and less well defended than Mycenae. Pisa was a full day's march away and their approach would doubtless be observed, but this seemed of no importance to Agamemnon. The image of Clytemnestra, never far from his thoughts, arose now ever brighter and added incentive to his mission.

Agamemnon rode out with his warriors, spearmen and archers ready for battle at sunrise. All I ever learned of this enterprise was that the Pisans resisted fiercely until Tantalus was cut down; some say by Agamemnon himself. He entered the palace, sought out Clytemnestra and dragged her away. It is claimed by some that he seized from her and killed her boy child, less than a month old, before her eyes. Do I believe this? I came to know what he, like his father, was capable of but surely not that. Surely not; yet still the question haunts me. What her thoughts, her feelings must have been either way I can barely imagine. Nevertheless, on returning to Mycenae it seems she came to accept her situation and little time passed before she and Agamemnon were married. News of what was alleged to have happened reached Tyndareus who was, of course, Clytemnestra's father. Hostilities between Sparta and Mycenae might have been expected but there were none. This was because Tyndareus, getting on in years and having adopted Agamemnon's brother, Menelaus, as his son and successor, was concerned to preserve the alliance with Mycenae and decided to forgive its king. Also, he regarded Agamemnon's marriage to his daughter as resulting in a better arrangement than that he'd had with Tantalus.

Clytemnestra enjoyed, or should I say willingly accepted, the luxuries of a Mycenaean queen, though her resentment of Agamemnon can have slept but lightly and must always have followed her as a shadow and haunted her thoughts in the depths of night. As you might have expected she soon began to bear children. First was her daughter, Chrysothemis, followed by Iphigenia, with the third being me, then after two more years, her son Orestes –

yes, she was *my* mother also and from now on that's how I will refer to her.

Chapter 2
My Life Begins

I was born into that much troubled House of Atreus and raised by my mother's attendants, sometimes by her, and on rare occasions I was aware of my father's presence when he loomed large over me. I was barely eight years old when I heard about Troy. Yes, it was a year when great matters were afoot – matters that those above me thought were no concern of mine. Even so, quiet and unobtrusive as I usually was at that tender age, I listened and I remembered what I heard over the years from many mouths, from those in the palace and others who passed through, from some who whispered and some, who thinking themselves secure in their pronouncements, allowed others to hear their words. Much of what I heard I at first did not fully understand but later all would become clearer. Memory is a deep well but I find the waters of mine not unduly darkened.

You will recall how Tyndareus of Sparta took my uncle, Menelaus, as his adopted son and successor. Menelaus married the beautiful Helen and all seemed well for a while though it turned out the gods, being bored with eternity as they very often are, went about adding further to the mischief in our lands.

Tyndareus had been dead for some time and Menelaus was king when Paris, a son of King Priam, ruler of Troy, arrived at Sparta with his companions. Paris had been sent as an envoy to address ever present disputes over trade and taxes imposed by the Trojans upon shipping that attempted to sail through the Hellespont on its way east to trade for grain. Hearing of his approach, people gathered in the streets of Sparta to deliver verbal abuse but the Trojan prince was well guarded against violence. Once enjoying palace hospitality, Paris soon was quite bewitched by the alluring Helen and so persuaded Menelaus to let him extend his stay in Sparta where he and his small group would be suitably entertained. Helen took full advantage of the Trojan prince's ill-disguised passions when Menelaus was out hunting or otherwise involved and they soon were meeting in secret. If Menelaus had any idea as to what was going on between Paris and his wife he chose to ignore it, perhaps knowing how fickle was her behaviour and expecting Paris would soon leave the city. Gossip was, however, already spreading throughout the Spartan court where its people held scant respect for the Trojan.

Then a fatal co-incidence - or did the gods ordain this also? Another envoy arrived one morning, this time from the famed palace of Knossos on Crete with a message for Menelaus from her king, Idomeneus. The message this man bore had Menelaus sailing off with the envoy next morning to the funeral, so it was first claimed, of a dear friend on Crete. Apparently he departed with no more fuss than he might when out for a day's hunting. It's said Menelaus also looked forward to being entertained amidst the luxuries of Knossos and the pleasures of its women. More importantly, there was also talk of a Cretan princess and some kind of alliance on offer which would greatly enhance the prestige of Sparta and her king since the navies of Knossos, though not as powerful as they once were, still controlled much of the seas thereabouts and continued in their efforts to suppress piracy. Idomeneus, grandson of the legendary King Minos, had also been a suitor of Helen though never having visited Sparta his image of her was based solely upon the reports of his agents. Menelaus' vessel had barely put to sea before the court began to discuss openly what his wife and the Trojan had been up to although the vapours of gossip had already flowed into the town. Later in the day, roused by members of the court, an armed mob, many of them seafaring men, approached the palace threatening to murder Paris if he didn't quit Sparta, such was their respect for Menelaus but more so their attitude towards Troy, which most saw as a hated enemy. Paris and his attendants fled Sparta in fear the very evening of the day Menelaus departed – and Paris took Helen with him.

You may think, as did I, that Menelaus had been influenced by those above who guide and so often manipulate our actions, if not then the King of Sparta must have been dangerously naïve. On his return almost a month later he was furious at having been so easily duped. He maintained his wife must have been abducted by Paris and his men, rather than her leaving Sparta willingly, and so Menelaus regarded this as an act of war. He rode straight away to Mycenae where he discussed matters with his brother, Agamemnon. As tensions between Troy and much of Greece had simmered for many years with minor hostile incidents, now had occurred a good enough excuse for the Greeks to rally their forces. The prospect of a major conflict appealed greatly to my father as king of the wealthiest, most powerful and influential city state in the entire region. He promptly dispatched envoys not just throughout the Peloponnese but northwards into Thessaly, westwards into Attica and Euboea then as far as the islands of the south-east Aegean and to Crete itself. His plan, one to which most acceded, was open war with the destruction of Troy its ultimate goal.

To organise such an enterprise would of course take months. The abduction of Menelaus' wife might to some have meant little but most of those approached by the envoys regarded the prospect of curbing the power of Troy and gaining plunder from the city itself as well as from her allies with enthusiasm. All those contributing men and vessels agreed to assemble at the port of Aulis on the east coast of Boeotia where sacrifices would be made before setting sail east. First they would attack some of Troy's allies on the Aegean coast, replenish their supplies then continue north to the city itself. It has since been claimed that there were as many as a thousand ships assembled at Aulis but others assure me this number has been somewhat inflated by the passage of time. It must nevertheless have been a mighty fleet.

But mighty fleet or no the winds proved mightier still and prevented their departure. The turn of the year was not a good time for sea voyages with frequent heavy rain adding further misery. Many days passed without any sign of the storm easing. Supplies were diminished with several crews becoming restless and some voicing their intention to return home overland if things did not improve. It began to look as if the whole enterprise might fail until Agamemnon's soothsayer, an old priest called Calchas, began to proclaim retribution from the gods as being the cause of the storm because Agamemnon, who from now on I will refer to as my father had, when out hunting, had killed a stag sacred to the goddess Artemis. The answer, Calchas claimed, had to be a greater sacrifice than any so far offered – that of Iphigenia, one of – yes, one of my *own* sisters! Under different circumstances Calchas' pronouncements might have been dismissed out of hand but here they offered hope and most of the men appeared to believe what he said was true because they wanted it to be so. My father as leader of the expedition had to be seen to comply, however reluctantly, with the prophecy because many, especially those who had never before encountered Calchas, believed he had some success when it came to foretelling the future. I never heard why he chose Iphigenia when my other sister, Chrysothemis, was already there. Chrysothemis had joined the fleet to be with the much admired Achilles who, though old enough to be her father, was thought might marry her in spite of her being hardly more than a child. He was also said to have expressed his admiration for Iphigenia and myself after a recent visit to Mycenae. His muscular presence and deep, boastful voice may have impressed many but not, I must confess, me. An empty amphora, it is said, makes most noise.

My father sent a party of horsemen hurrying back overland to fetch Iphigenia on the pretext of marrying *her* off to Achilles instead of Chrysothemis but during the delay he prayed hard and offered sacrifice to Poseidon hoping the weather would change before his daughter showed up – but it did not. Four days later, when the party returned with Iphigenia, our mother had made the journey with her. Father was horrified as the sacrifice was planned to take place after dark at the temple of Artemis on the day Iphigenia arrived so our mother learned of it straight away. She pleaded hard with father, she begged on her knees in pouring rain for him not to go ahead with the sacrifice but he had her removed from his presence. Circumstances demanded the sacrifice had to happen – or was believed by all to have happened. Others unknown who pitied Iphigenia and hated Calchas, a small group close to the king himself, devised a plan to make it appear that it had. Strong winds and heavy rain in utter darkness helped to disguise the act. There were screams and sobs when the priest so appointed raised his knife – the voice of Iphigenia herself so it was thought, and it sounded genuine enough to those close enough to hear because she who played the part really had to convince them all her throat was about to be cut. It was convincing also to our mother who'd been held back forcibly with the rest of the crowd. The real victim, however, was a small deer that left enough blood on the altar to allay the doubts next morning of anyone who cared to go and look. And many did.

Amazingly, and most probably to the relief of Calchas whose life may well have depended upon it, the skies did brighten early the following day, then the winds calmed and shifted in favour of the waiting vessels. On seeing this, one of those involved in the deception summoned the courage to confide in father over what had really happened at the alleged sacrifice. On learning the truth I believe father, much relieved by it, had intended to tell mother that Iphigenia was alive and well but she'd had her escort leave Aulis that same night and rush her in despair back to Mycenae before he was able to do that. He couldn't have sent a messenger after her, either, without risk of revealing the deception to others, including his own men and Calchas, who might preach retribution from the vengeful immortals who so often inflict that kind of thing. Two days later the fleet had set sail for Troy.

Iphigenia, meanwhile, had been escorted in secret, well clear of the camp and sent on her journey to an out of the way place called Tauris, many days distant. She was supposed to stay in hiding there at another temple dedicated to Artemis until after father and the rest of the fleet had sailed, then return to Mycenae. As I only much later was to learn, she chose to remain a trainee priestess at Tauris without letting anyone there know who she really was. After all, she was aware her own father had sanctioned her death. And who could blame her for wishing to leave behind for good our maladjusted family?

Our mother, knowing no more of this at the time than did I and the rest of our court, explained to me in tearful anguish what she thought had happened to Iphigenia so I was naturally distraught. And what did my six years old brother, Orestes, feel when he learned about the event as our mother related it? I knew he was unhappy for a time but did not fully understand what was going on and said little. I remained saddened and confused and I cried each night for many days afterwards. It left Orestes, and me without the company or support of the other girls. At least he had his toys, a wooden sword and a small chariot with which he engaged in noisy war games with other boys; in particular with his friend Pylades who was within a month his own age. Yes, their often proclaimed goal was to become fierce warriors when they were old enough and Orestes would dash about waving his little wooden sword around as if ready to engage in some imaginary battle, shouting, "Hi-ho, here I go!"

Orestes, of course, was too young by far to assert any kind of authority so our mother ended up carrying the main burden of palace business. It was a responsibility she hardly cared for from the beginning but she cared even less for the disputes and interference in palace affairs by the city elders or noble courtiers, many of them owners of workshops within the palace or land beyond the city wall. Ruling a kingdom, as you will understand, was considered a man's - a fighting man's job, but she had no intention of letting this daunt her and it was expected Agamemnon would not be away for more than a year at most. It was never made obvious in conversation but I sensed within her the bitter hatred of a husband who she believed had sanctioned the ritual murder of one of her young daughters. For a time she was sullen, leaving us to the care of attendants and slaves. There were few visitors to the court as so many men had sailed away to Troy, though only a bit less activity in the megaron where music played and the remaining male and usual female courtiers continued to indulge their business as well as their pleasures. I and my friends, sometimes joined by Orestes, occupied ourselves in chasing about parts of the palace seldom used except for storage, playing hide and seek with some of the younger slaves. There we'd make fanciful wagers over who would be first to spot a rat, or more reassuringly, a cat. My brother would now and again pretend he'd seen something much worse so as to scare us out of our wits. Little Orestes, though, began to spend more of his time with members of the palace guard, usually with Pylades, in watching them practise their deadly arts and continued to assert how he yearned one day for the life of a warrior.

**

The first year went by, then two more with no news from my father or of the fortunes of any who had sailed for Troy under his leadership. There was hearsay from traders who had passed through the Hellespont but none, seeing the city under siege, had dared to approach Troy. In all that time I never again heard my mother, mention Iphigenia and she seldom referred to my father or the enterprise of Troy unless another person prompted the subject. Orestes by now was inclined to spend much of his daylight time outside the city wall in that area allocated for training in combat. I on occasion would set out with my female attendants and a pair of male slaves to see what he was about. Only a small number of palace guards, their ranks depleted for obvious reasons, could be there at any one time and with these Orestes had begun to practise his use of the sword - by now a real sword of sharpened bronze, and his potential skills in archery where the target was usually a dead pig suspended from a pole. At nine years of age he was not yet big and strong enough to carry one of the large, figure of eight shields borne by fully grown warriors though he and Pylades sometimes grappled with the things; each laughing at the antics of the other. On those infrequent occasions when an envoy arrived at court to announce the coming of a delegation from another city, Orestes now and again attended the megaron to listen to what was said and there witness the customary exchange of gifts. And although I was expected to remain in the background I was seldom far away.

Other less formal commitments involved our mother dealing with the petty affairs of supplicants, complainants, slaves and criminals as well as others about the palace who already had their allocated tasks. At night I sometimes dismissed those appointed to watch over me then hurry down to meet my brother in the anteroom of the megaron. If we didn't go outside we would prowl through corridors, some lit by burning brands, others not. What we were looking for I never really knew, nor did Orestes. Some lurking demon, perhaps. But it was quite exciting at the time to pretend something sinister might be waiting in the shadows, as we had in those earlier childhood games. One night we heard footsteps approach and we hid together behind a column as the sounds grew closer. A man went by and we saw his face momentarily illuminated by a firebrand. It was Periphas, the captain of our palace guard, a stocky man with a scarred face. When he'd passed us by we tip-toed quietly after him up the steps to the floor above. Soon enough he stopped at a door, tapped and entered. It was our mother's private chamber. After that we stayed away for fear of being discovered.

Then one morning, when the third year had ended, as rain clouds sullied our skies and fires burned brighter within the great hall to retain warmth, a stranger appeared at our court. At least he was a stranger to me as I sat on a plinth by mother's throne, and a stranger he would at first be to Orestes. The newcomer was a tall, slim man of young to middle years with shoulder-length black hair and short beard. His attire was that of a minor noble but one well-travelled and therefore in appearance not so well kept. He wore at his side an ornate scabbard in which rested a sword that appeared, from the quality of its hilt, to be of finest craftsmanship. He had himself conducted before our mother by two members of the palace guard and there was introduced, attracting only moderate attention from those few courtiers present. Being at

43

the time close to her throne I well recall his first words, delivered with a bow: "Lady Clytemnestra, my name is Aegisthus, son of Thyestes, brother of Atreus who once ruled here."

"Oh, really," she replied after some hesitation, "I have heard much about you but your name is not well spoken of here in Mycenae and nor is that of Thyestes. You and your father are said to have murdered Atreus so what is your intended business with us?"

The two guards stood ready to evict him and mother continued to stare hard as he replied, "Only of late did I hear about the expedition sailing against Troy with Agamemnon your king and husband as their leader. There were unfortunate misunderstandings between Atreus and my father, and - ."

"Misunderstandings!" she cut in, half rising from her seat. "You murdered Atreus then your father seized this very throne and ruled here until Agamemnon evicted him. I ask you again and for the last time – what is your intended business here?"

Prompted by the harsh tone of her voice, the two guards moved closer still to Aegisthus, ready to take hold and drag him forcibly from the hall. My mother relaxed, continued to stare and waited for his answer.

"I – I and my five companions have travelled much but only recently was I told of your misfortunes; of the death at Artemis' altar of your daughter, Iphigenia, and the heavy burden of leadership that has fallen upon you since Agamemnon departed for Troy. Lady Clytemnestra,

I know well the workings of the palace and as I'm not otherwise occupied I wondered if I might be of service here until your husband returns. You must know as well, with so many fighting men absent, there have been incursions of pirates. Many coastal towns have been attacked and some unable to hold out against these brigands."

"The walls of Mycenae are strong," she informed him, tersely. "And this is no coastal fishing town. And I take it you are without enough of value to support yourself."

"That, er, that is true," he answered, "but the villages and farms hereabout, your livestock, olive groves and orchards – all may be vulnerable to these incursions after the winter winds have passed. Why not let my few men act as the eyes of Mycenae and join to assist the men of your palace guard should this be necessary? Agamemnon and I never crossed swords so I ask you to believe me when I say I bare no ill-will against this house. Should I not prove to be of good service then I will rightly expect dismissal."

Even at eleven years old I was aware of the impression this man was making on my mother. He was, as I better appreciated in later years, a handsome man as well as being one possessed of courtly speech and manners. My mother appeared for a time lost for a response and the crack of settling timbers in the hearth emphasised her silence. When she spoke she averted her gaze for some moments as though fearing Aegisthus might ascertain her thoughts.

"You must -," she said at last, "you must allow me to think over your words. For now I will have food and wine prepared for you and you'll be shown somewhere to rest." With this she nodded to the guards who turned and gestured for Aegisthus to follow them. As he was escorted from the megaron she looked down at me to ask, "Well, my darling, what did you think of that man? Have you heard him spoken of before?"

"I've heard others mention him, that's all," I replied, taking a deep breath, which had her waiting for me to say more. I looked up then added, "I don't like him, mother. I don't know why – I just don't."

She considered my answer then replied, "I understand but – but I need someone able to deal with those tiresome day to day affairs that were once handled by those who followed your father to Troy. And what he says about pirates may well be true; yes, I'm hearing much more about them of late and the seas will eventually be calmer than they are now. No one remaining with us here is as well suited as that man Aegisthus, or so I think. I will offer him the opportunity to relieve me of some of the many burdens I carry but the other men he mentions as having travelled with him I will not allow to stay in Mycenae; they're probably no better than the brigands he mentioned so I will have them housed outside the city wall. Do try to be pleasant to him, won't you, dear; he may prove useful in the end."

I remember nodding my acquiescence but barely did I understand just then how her mind was working. Having that man help lighten her palace duties and maintain a watch beyond the city wall were not the only considerations to liven her mind. I understood later how desirable a woman our mother still was and that cannot have escaped our newcomer's thoughts.

***

Aegisthus, accorded his own rooms in the palace, took up residence and soon after was allocated a pair of female slaves. As the months passed his presence became ever more familiar in the great hall and to our mother's readily expressed satisfaction, he took on responsibility for overseeing many mundane tasks that previously had weighed upon her. She granted him the attire of a Mycenaean palace noble so that his authority would be found more acceptable, in particular to those remaining occupants of the palace who remembered him from during the brief but bloody reign of Thyestes.

By then I was of the opinion that Aegisthus coveted the throne of Mycenae and considered the presence upon it of a woman, almost unheard of throughout Greece, to turn out sooner or later in his favour. Did our mother suspect this? I believe now she did and planned to use him as long as it suited her purposes – one being rather personal as it transpired.

As the months passed, as his authority became ever more established, Aegisthus began to take his evening meals and wine with our mother. This was for a time in the dining hall next to the megaron but later in the privacy of the chamber where our father held discussion with the visiting worthies and rulers of other towns and cities. By the end of Aegisthus' first year in Mycenae, our mother had ordered another, though simpler throne of wood, set up in the megaron so that he could sit by her side, act as her consort, advise upon her decisions and listen to the words and the playing of Leucon, our bard.

"What's your opinion of Aegisthus?" I asked my brother one day after I had watched him and Pylades indulge with enthusiasm in a spell of more strenuous training – sword work, spear throwing, that sort of thing.

"I don't like him," he replied, tapping the hilt of his new sword. "He hardly ever smiles – always looks shifty and walks like he's drunk, which he probably is. I loathe him, really I do."

"Me too," I added. 'We both know what he's up to as well, don't we."

"Yes," Orestes agreed, "and I wish they'd stick him out here for target practice instead of the pig."

"And mother knows what he's up to, I'm sure of it," I added, "Each of them is planning to take advantage of the other, I'm sure about that as well. Mother at least has the palace guard to call upon and I don't think *they're* too keen on Aegisthus either."

"No, Electra, you're right, they don't like him at all; I've heard them say they don't."

"It's true," confirmed Pylades, "they don't like him one bit."

"And as we've seen," I added under my breath, "the captain shares her bed on occasion." Then, passing through my thoughts the words, "And I'm convinced Aegisthus also shares it when Periphas isn't around – yes, I'd be most surprised if he doesn't. Perhaps more often."

***

The flame of a small pottery oil lamp swayed gently on the opposite side of the room from their window. Beyond the widow a starlit night sky breathed warm air over the wool-softened bed to which they had earlier retired to indulge their pleasures.

'I'm told there were visitors today,' breathed Aegisthus, 'envoys perhaps. You've said nothing since I returned though there seemed to be much on your mind, even when we -. Was their visit of any importance? Perhaps I should have been here.'

'Perhaps, perhaps not,' replied Clytemnestra, gazing into the darkness of a timber-beamed ceiling. 'Two of them arrived while you were out hunting with that rabble of yours.'

'You still refer to those men as rabble but they've served me well through difficult times even if they're not accustomed to court manners.'

'I spotted them again today in the marketplace,' she said. 'They look more suited to digging ditches than bearing arms.' Both were silent for a while then Clytemnestra said, 'The men who arrived here today – they were from Troy.'

'From Troy!' he exclaimed sitting upright. 'Why did you not send for me? Are they still here in the palace?'

'They *are* still here in the palace and I didn't send for you because it was me and *me only* they expected to speak with. Yes, and it was only myself alone I wished them to see.'

'Oh, very well, but – but is there news of – of -
.'

'Of my husband, of Agamemnon; is that what you mean?'

'Yes, of course that's what I mean; I have to know about this, don't I. We need to be prepared if -
.'

'You appear to have forgotten,' she cut in angrily, sitting upright next to Aegisthus, 'I may on occasion share my bed with you but let's not forget that *I* still rule Mycenae and will continue to do so until -.'

'Until –? Is Agamemnon soon to return?'

'You can relax, dear; I gather from the envoys that Agamemnon, Menelaus and all their allies are still camped outside Troy with the plunder they'd collected on their way there. The Trojans have refused to negotiate or to return Menelaus' wife. Men have died on both sides but Agamemnon and his brother are well. They tell me neither side is able to defeat the other in battle and they have no idea how long the situation might last.'

'Oh, well that's – that's interesting. Perhaps we'll have more news in time.'

'Perhaps,' said Clytemnestra, settling back under the woollen blanket, 'so for now, my darling, you can rest in peace.'

***

I'd been sitting close by her throne earlier that day, listening to the lyre playing of old Leucon and singing to myself as I often do. When those men arrived mother seemed to have forgotten I was there, or maybe she thought it didn't matter if I was, so I listened quietly to all that was said. I left the palace as soon as the envoys had gone from the megaron and hurried off to find my brother. He was in his usual location, as so often with Pylades, learning how to kill people but grinning the way he usually did. This time he was casting his spear at a newly replaced yet already flyblown dead pig.

"Orestes!" I called. "We've had news from Troy!"

He handed his spear to one of the men involved in his training and strode manfully over to me, followed by his friend. "News – what news?" he asked. "Is father on his way back?"

"Not yet, no. They remain camped outside Troy and still not getting anywhere. That's what the messengers said. They told us that father is alive and well."

"That's not much of a message is it," shrugged Orestes. "And while he's still out there we're stuck with Aegisthus who sometimes acts as if he owns the place. Everyone knows by now he's often in bed with our mother, don't they. I wonder what the captain of our palace guard thinks of it. She used to favour him or so I thought."

"I'm not sure if she still does. I've noticed the way they look at each other when she summons him but in mother's case I doubt her feelings are genuine. It's only when Aegisthus isn't around, when he's away hunting with those men of his or with one of the slave girls. You'd have noticed if you weren't out here most of the day."

"I wonder," he smiled, "what would happen if both her men turned up on the same night."

51

"I really cannot imagine," I breathed.

"That could be fun," grinned Pylades.

"I wish Periphas would run the miserable bugger through," remarked Orestes. "I'd love to and one day maybe I will!" Orestes smiled again, tapped the sword at his side then added, "Well I suppose we'd better get on with a bit more practice – all we've killed so far today is the same dead pig. It's time we had a new one and I'll call it Aegisthus just like the others!"

"Well apart from killing dead pigs," I informed him, "there's something else you should turn your mind to."

"Really, what?"

"You should learn to read and to write, both of you, if it's not too late – you know, those tablets with messages and important records. Our father can read and write as well as kill people and so ought you, Orestes, if you want to succeed him; palace records are very important. There's not much use in our having scribes all over the place if you don't know what they've written."

"Well as it happens," he responded smugly, "that old goat of a slave you've maybe seen me talking to – he can read things and he's been showing us both how to do it. But I don't want other people knowing we have to depend on the likes of him or anyone else for *that* kind of thing." He tapped the sword once more and declared, "This is what I intend to be good at and I mean *really* good; Pylades here as well."

"That's right," Pylades agreed. Orestes friend was not one for too many words.

52

You may have gathered that being in their fourteenth year, both were at a difficult age with Orestes prone to boasting as he often did when referring to the times he spent training with his friend and sleeping out at night to harden his constitution. I considered, though, that his days and nights away from the palace were preferable to his spending time there when Aegisthus was around. And now my brother was showing interest in the younger girls of our court, as was Pylades, though neither was too fussy about their status. To this particular activity I feigned indifference although I couldn't imagine how it left either of them enough time to study tablets.

Maybe as a result of Orestes increasing absence, by that I mean his hardly ever being there, Aegisthus was more in evidence about the megaron. He was also more frequently to be seen seated next to mother, who appeared happy to accept his presence. I asked myself often how long it might be before our father got back to expel this intrusive man for good.

Chapter 3
The Return of Agamemnon

Six more years passed during which time my moods swung from hope to despair and back time and time again. Young as I was I should have expected suitors from all the great cities of the Peloponnese and beyond but few of even modest worth appeared as those who might have mattered were still away at Troy. News from Troy had been frustratingly sparse until the fifth year when events were reported that gave myself and my brother some hope of our father's return. This time we were informed how the great hero Achilles had been killed by an arrow shot by Paris, the man who had fled from Sparta with Helen, and how he in turn had been slain in similar manner. Yes, it seemed at last, with Troy possibly getting the worst of things our time of waiting might at long last be over.

Orestes was approaching full manhood, already a fine athletic figure with shoulder-length, fair hair, less boastful now yet fully confident in his abilities as a fighting man. It was obvious before then that he ought to have been by our mother's side in the great hall and not Aegisthus who I avoided whenever possible. On numerous occasions in the palace, in corridor or anteroom when no one else was around, Aegisthus had approached me to ask with more or less the same words, "Why don't you join me for a cup of wine? I know you still don't accept my presence here but this is simply through misunderstandings. Will you not for once agree?"

I didn't care to antagonise the man especially when, as so often, he'd consumed too much wine, so I usually countered his question with, "No, I feel it is not in my interest or my place to do so. You must excuse me."

One day, when Aegisthus was absent, I confronted mother in her private chamber and asked, "Why must you keep that awful man here when Orestes should instead be your consort?"

"I have discussed his continuing presence with Orestes on more than one occasion," she replied, "and explained to him the situation as you yourself know it. Aegisthus I much rely upon because he has a sound knowledge of affairs in which Orestes has taken almost no interest. Your brother is seldom here except to involve himself with the girls and prefers otherwise to be out hunting wild boar, deer or whatever with that friend of his, as well as showing others how good he now is with spear and bow. Let me assure you, when your father returns things will be different."

"And what becomes of your precious Aegisthus when father does return? I take it you'll be getting rid of him and that won't be too soon, either, because I abhor the way he keeps looking at me and tries to involve me in conversation. He sometimes lays a hand on my arm and that makes my flesh crawl. He wants to have both mother and daughter, I know it! I'm surprised you're not aware of his pestering me, really I am."

"No, dear, I confess I hadn't really noticed because he wouldn't do so if I was there, but I'll speak to him about it anyway. Perhaps for the time being you should avoid wearing the usual dress of a court woman as that might all the more attract his attention." This I accepted though she, leaving her own breasts exposed, suited her well enough. "And to answer your other question," she continued, "I dare say when Agamemnon returns Aegisthus will be offered another responsibility - or obliged to leave."

I wasn't convinced over much of what she'd said so I went to talk to my brother who of course knew even less of all mother had claimed than I did. But then, who else could I speak with. As so often I found him outside the city with those other men, this time engaged in swordplay with a small circular shield at his left arm. Unfortunately, in spite of his declared loathing of Aegisthus, he was happy with the freedom he'd become used to and preferred to await the return home of our father for whom he at least had retained some respect, albeit respect of a handed down image. I didn't find his attitude at all comforting because the fleet had sailed for Troy almost ten years before and the war seemed interminable.

Then, late in my seventeenth year, it happened. The weather was inclement so that day I remained largely within the megaron. I was seated with friends on the edge of the circular hearth, close to the comforting warmth and life of the fire and some way from the throne where mother presided, for once without the company of Aegisthus. We were chattering, indulging ourselves with honeyed wine and pastries while old Leucon played his lyre, when two men were conducted into the hall. One was the envoy sent from Troy, the man who had previously visited us and was known also through the staff of office he carried. The other man, limping slightly from what appeared to be a wound to his right foot, was dressed as a warrior of some distinction with bronze corselet, sword at his side and a plumed bronze helmet which he removed when standing before my bare-breasted mother. On this as on most other occasions she was happy to display that part of a firm, slim and curvaceous body many women of lesser years would have been proud to possess. The newcomers' arrival struck me as being of such importance that I whispered to one of my girls, "Go and fetch Orestes - you know where he is. Go now - quickly." Then I arose and stepped over to hear what the newcomers had to say.

"Lady Clytemnestra," the envoy began, "I bring to you and to Mycenae great and wonderful news. Troy has at last fallen and her king, Priam, is slain. King Agamemnon will by now have set sail and in three days' time will come ashore with his men to the south of here and pass through the territory of our ally, Argos. This man I bring into your presence is Philoctetes who witnessed far more than I am able to tell, if you wish now to hear him."

She did not rise from the throne but stared at bristle-faced, shaggy haired Philoctetes for some moments then said, "Yes, I would indeed like to hear what he has to say." She called for wine, relaxed and listened intently, as did I while sitting discreetly by the column close her throne.

"Lady Clytemnestra," he began, "Firstly, King Agamemnon is well an' in good spirits though many of our men 'ave fallen before the walls of Troy includin' Achilles who was killed by Paris, the man many believe was cause of the conflict."

"This we have earlier been told," said my mother.

"Aye, madam, but it was I who in turn slew Paris with an arrow shot of my own an' of that I'm proud. But it was another who is said to 'ave sealed the fate of the Trojans by trickery; one Odysseus, King of Ithaca, a small island of no great importance north of the Peloponnese. It was claimed to be 'is idea that our men, strange as this may seem, construct a great wooden monument outside of Troy in the shape of an 'orse. Work began at once though it took best part of a month with armed parties goin' to an' fro to cut timbers in the forests and with much sawin' an' 'ammerin'. When completed the thing looked more like an ox than an 'orse, and it stood facin' directly the main gate of the city."

"And what was the point in all of that?" Clytemnestra asked as filled goblets were handed out from a bronze tray by her female slave. "I imagine the Trojans must have asked very much the same question."

"Aye, they must indeed an' so might I 'ave at first. They watched from the walls with great interest an' much amusement. Soon after the thing was completed our men gathered up their arms and those of our dead, made their sacrifices to Zeus an' Poseidon then returned to their vessels. At first light, with great ceremony and singin', they set sail and left the shores of Troy."

There followed an expectant silence while Philoctetes drank then a further brief delay when Orestes entered and crossed the megaron to sit by me. I thought mother might have introduced him to Philoctetes but she didn't. At the same time I noticed movement to my left. Several steps away, part hidden in shadow by a column, Aegisthus stood watching and listening.

"The Trojans," Philoctetes continued, "must 'ave assumed that after all those years without 'avin' breached their city wall we'd at last given up and sailed off 'ome. The gods, accordin' to our soothsayers, includin' Calchas 'ad, 'owever, turned against the Trojans. For one thing, this very same Odysseus 'ad some days earlier persuaded the Trojans to let 'im into their town disguised as an escaped slave or prisoner. Once in there he'd stole that which the Trojans most valued, the Palladium, a wooden image of a maiden supposed to 'ave been sent by the gods as a pledge for the safety of Troy but only for as long as it remained within the city. He escaped with it at night. It was this same Odysseus, together with 'andful of armed men, includin' myself, who entered at night an' remained concealed within the wooden 'orse. After ten years under siege the Trojans regarded our departure as worthy of a great celebration an' so they set aside all caution. They threw open their main gate and, regardin' the 'orse as a kind of trophy they 'auled it into the city an' closed the gate be'ind as if worried someone might steal it. Fires were lit, meat cooked an' countless jars of wine from Priam's palace made available to all of Troy's citizens. Some there wished to break up the 'orse or worse still, set it ablaze – we bein' inside it could 'ear 'em say so an' we feared we might be 'acked to death or burned alive, aye, that we did. But Priam ordered that it should be preserved an' 'ad guards placed there to protect it."

"Were these people not stupid?" asked Clytemnestra. "Did none of them consider what this wooden horse might be? Not a gift from the gods, surely."

"With the Palladium gone," replied Philoctetes, "their minds were turned by touch of the gods an' by strong Trojan wine. If they'd sent someone out to watch our men leave they might 'ave observed our ships not to sail far out to sea but to steer some modest distance along the coast to where they found moorin's in a secluded bay. That night our vessels returned unobserved to their shores an' our men, all fully armed, disembarked before sunrise. This Odysseus, meanwhile, 'ad opened the belly of the wooden 'orse an' with the rest of us 'ad descended from it. We slew those left to guard it who were too drunk to know what was 'appenin', then we reopened the main city gate for our men to enter." He drank deeply from his goblet then hesitated as though recalling in full all that had happened that day. "Aye, they rushed in unopposed. The slaughter was terrible; all those years of pent up frustration expressed itself with sharpened bronze an' everywhere ran with the blood of men, women an' even children. The very walls of the city cried out in agony, I swear they did. We seized much plunder, many precious goods an' younger women. Agamemnon took away with 'im Cassandra, a daughter of Priam, one said to foretell the future, though it seems she'd not been successful in so doin' before the city fell. As our vessels departed with pennants flyin' I watched Troy burn beneath rollin' clouds of vengeance. We sailed away proud but when our vessels entered open seas we were struck by a storm. The gods preserved us all – except for the vessels of Odysseus. When the weather cleared they were gone from sight an' we saw nothin' of 'em again."

Silence descended while those around considered his words, then, "I thank you for the gratifying account you have given us," said Clytemnestra. "But now you both must take food and rest while I discuss with others all you have said."

Hearing the words of Philoctetes seemed to open a new door for my sixteen years old brother. As two of Clytemnestra's attendants ushered her visitors away he arose, stepped up to the vacant seat by her throne and said, "Mother, I must take my place by your side until father arrives here. I should have done so before you allowed that man Aegisthus into you presence. I will in future try to play my part as I should."

"You do surprise me, dear," she responded. "I'm sure your father will be delighted."

61

To me her words sounded hollow but I remained silent. On turning aside, I observed Aegisthus quietly leaving the megaron.

***

'I heard all that was said,' announced Aegisthus as he joined Clytemnestra in her private chambers after sunset. 'Three days, that man told you. Three days before Agamemnon is back here. We must decide very soon what we're to do.'

'There is only one answer,' she said quietly, 'one and one alone.'

'What d'you mean?'

'You know perfectly well what I mean - do we *have* to pretend? And you know as well as I what would happen if Agamemnon found you here. He'd cut you into pieces and feed you to the dogs.'

Aegisthus stared at her, drank a little wine then said, 'Yes, quite; and no, we don't have to pretend, do we. But the palace guard are loyal and await Agamemnon's return, we both know that. And they're also loyal to his son – your son, Orestes, are they not.'

'After ten years they are loyal by and large only to my husband's memory,' she breathed, 'a memory kept alive mainly by their captain, Periphas, who was my husband's staunch and trusted companion. Agamemnon didn't want him to go to Troy in case there were problems needing to be dealt with here. As for Orestes, yes, he plays his war games with some of Periphas' men but I much doubt they see him as rising to the throne of Mycenae for some time to come.'

'So – then what exactly have you in mind?'

'Those men of yours you claim followed you all around Greece,' Clytemnestra replied, 'I take it they still reside outside the city wall.'

'Yes, I manage to keep them supplied with gold pieces, though much of that is squandered at the inns on those occasions when they do enter the city.'

'*My* gold, you mean, Aegisthus, dear. *That* is what you keep them with.'

'Er, yes, *your* gold.'

'And I've ignored the fact that they have entered Mycenae on numerous nights against my wishes as you well know. But now I think we'll have them enter the city and the palace with my full consent and I believe you know what has to be done. Periphas intends to visit me here tomorrow after darkness has fallen – do you understand?'

'Yes, I understand,' muttered Aegisthus under his breath. 'I know what has to be done.'

***

It was midmorning and I was seated by the great hearth in the megaron with my friends when an agitated, wide-eyed Orestes came hurrying in. Our mother wasn't present so, he headed straight over to me.

"What's the matter – what's happened?" I asked as he sat close by.

"It's Periphas!" he gasped. "He's dead – murdered!"

His words shocked me. I didn't at first believe him. I didn't believe him because I didn't want to believe him. "What d'you mean, murdered?" I asked, grasping his arm.

"Murdered," he repeated. "I was with some of his men as usual outside the city wall when this peasant came over to say he'd gone to rescue a stray sheep and found a body in the valley below the palace. I went down there with the rest of them to take a look and it's definitely him – yeah, definitely Periphas."

I stared hard at Orestes, as those words burned into me. I was still thinking it couldn't be true – still hoping it was someone else he'd seen. "Murdered?" I asked him. "How d'you know he's been murdered – tell me, how?"

"He must have fallen from the city wall but – but he's been stabbed many times about his body. He's all twisted and soaked in blood and his neck's broken; I could see that."

I continued to stare horrified, not knowing what more to say, then Orestes said, "I wonder what we're going to do?"

"Do," I responded, "I – I don't know. What *can* we do?" I looked at the empty throne, as did Orestes, and I wondered where our mother was. I had asked my friends to leave us so that I could talk further with Orestes when she appeared at the far end of the hall with, walking a few paces behind her, Aegisthus, who stared straight ahead. Orestes and I got up and stepped across to meet her but it was my brother who asked, "Do you know about Periphas being killed?"

She and Aegisthus halted and mother answered, "Yes, I was told a short time ago. That is – that is terrible news. We must find out what happened."

Aegisthus ignored us and I no more took our mother's response as truth then than I had earlier. How could she have known so soon when Orestes and the men he trained with had only just found out? But Orestes surprised me greatly in those tense moments when he announced to her, "Then as I said earlier, it's about time you had my support. From now on I'll sit by your side as the king's son ought to and father will find me here when he returns."

The gods must have been in him because having spoken so boldly he stepped over to the plinth where the thrones stood. There he adjusted his scabbard and seated himself in the lesser seat close to hers where Aegisthus so often took up his position and doubtless was expecting to do so then. Mother appeared startled then forced a smile as she walked over to join Orestes. I saw Aegisthus' face darken as he turned away without a word and strode from the megaron. Seated now in regal comfort, mother looked aside at Orestes and with the smile set firmly as baked clay she called over one of her personal slave girls and ordered wine. From the way she stared at me, whatever she and my brother were about to discuss was not intended for my ears, so I left to find my friends and talk about what had happened. Orestes and I would be together later. My thoughts returned to Periphas and to who might have served to bring about his death. One name and one name only stalked me as a dark shadow. It could be no other.

***

Morning sunlight was yet to pierce the window of the private chambers set aside to accommodate visitors of note as she sat in conversation with Aegisthus. 'I have informed all throughout our court via the palace guard that when Agamemnon enters the palace all mention of your name and presence is forbidden. Should anyone disobey, slave or courtier, I have instructed our men to ensure I never see that person again and I *do* mean never. After this is over you will take Periphas' place as head of the guard.'

'Head of the - will they accept me?'

'They must do so as you are directly answerable to me and it's my words and mine only that you will deliver to them unless circumstances dictate otherwise.'

'Then all is in place,' breathed Aegisthus, raising his goblet.

'All is in place,' agreed Clytemnestra, drinking from hers.

'And what about Orestes?'

'What d'you mean, what about Orestes? You're not suggesting we – no, he is my son after all.'

'But' Aegisthus insisted, 'things could become rather difficult, if you know what I mean.'

'I know perfectly well what you mean but we'll have to deal with matters as and when they arise and *that* you have to accept.'

'Yes, I suppose I must,' Aegisthus muttered.

Clytemnestra was about to call for more wine when hurried footsteps were heard approaching on the steps outside. The footsteps ceased and a breathless voice from beyond the closed door called, 'My Lady, I have news of vessels approaching!'

Clytemnestra arose, stepped over and pulled open the door to face one of her male attendants. 'Well,' she demanded, 'tell me all you've seen.'

'There are many vessels approaching Argos from the south; they must have lain offshore until the sky lightened. I did not stay long enough to count their number in such poor light but rode here at once. But pennants were flying – I could see many, many pennants. They will already be putting men ashore then they'll be on their way here.'

'Very well,' she said, coolly, 'you may go now.' She turned to Aegisthus, saying, 'Agamemnon may be with us before the sun has set so I have much to do. I will have a party of men sent out to greet them with horses, chariots and wagons, I will send out criers to have it proclaimed throughout Mycenae that Agamemnon will be with us this very day and I will order a banquet prepared in the dining hall for tonight. You must remain where you are and keep your nerve. Have yourself more wine and I'm sure you can summon a girl or two for company until I send for you.'

'And then what? For how long am I supposed to hide up here? I need to know!'

'Like I said, Aegisthus, dear,' she responded coldly, her eyes hard upon him, 'you stay up here until *I* send for you.'

He watched Clytemnestra leave, waited several heartbeats then arose with a hand resting hard against his sword hilt. Stepping to the door where outside waited a willowy, mop-haired male slave, he snapped, 'Fetch me a jug of wine and be quick about it!'

The youth pitter-pattered down, his bare feet treading cold steps. He returned a while later with the requested amphora, its weight as much as he could bear as he clutched it to his chest. With the vessel placed before him, Aegisthus dismissed the boy and reached for his goblet, muttering, 'I serve that woman well in more ways than one and still I'm treated like a damned outsider when I've as much at stake as she has – maybe more, maybe my very life!' He tilted the wine jug over his cup, poured liberally then muttered, 'This will not do. No, it will not.' He considered her suggestion that he indulge himself with female company but decided this was intended only to keep him where he was. Aegisthus raised the goblet and drank. And when the goblet was empty he refilled it.

On stepping ashore Agamemnon had sent ahead messengers to announce their coming so crowds were already gathered on rooftops and about the city wall. Light from a lowering sun glinted upon bronze arms and armour, drums were beating loudly and ram's horn sounded raucous notes as they drew nearer. It was plain to see riding ahead of the host in his gilded chariot the figure of King Agamemnon, his attire, though sullied by time and circumstance, well proclaiming his regal status. Following on horseback or in chariot were his close companions with horsehair plumes swaying proudly above helmets of varied shape and form. And behind these, on foot, armed and armoured men of the king's company together with rumbling wagons that contained the plunder of Troy and of her allies. Some wagons bore also captives fortunate, perhaps through their age or gender, to have survived the slaughter and flames in their home town. Many of those warriors on foot had already parted from the host and others were dispersing, all anxious to regain the homes they had so many years ago abandoned.

The drums and horns continued, now closer, now louder but with the men keeping their distance on level ground some way below the city wall. Spears were raised high, swords clashed against shields while the townsfolk of Mycenae waved and cheered, some crying aloud, 'There is our king!' and 'Oh, look, our king is returning!' The triumphant yet much depleted legion, faces turned toward the city proceeded on, skirting its formidable defensive wall, which they followed around until reaching the north side. There, with the sun already set, they approached the main portal of Mycenae, the Lion Gate. The imposing sculpture it displayed rested upon a massive stone lintel beneath which, led by Agamemnon, the royal party began to pass with some warriors following the high walls on the inner side while yet more dispersed to their longed for homes. Armed guards of the palace, firebrands raised in salute, held back clamouring crowds as Agamemnon and his boastful companions turned toward, entered and continued along the great stone ramp that led upwards and above part of the city before bearing left in its approach to the palace buildings.

On steps before the main entrance stood a smiling Clytemnestra in richly gowned, bear-breasted glory, her long fair hair pinned back by ornate, gilded clips. About her were gathered a select number of likewise attired female courtiers as well as plainly dressed slaves; these latter fallen to their knees but readied to do the bidding of the king or any of his close companions. To one side, unnoticed by Agamemnon, stood Orestes, eager to see a father who had departed Mycenae when he was but six years old. A few steps further back had assembled the gown-clutching, head-nodding city elders, nobles and priests. The drums and ram's horns had ceased but from within the palace flowed the inviting sound of pipes. The long-bearded, bear-like Agamemnon, his eyes set bright within a mask of weathered weariness framed by dark hair that cascaded unkempt below his broad shoulders, ascended with slave boys following to hold his sullied gown clear of the steps. His dedicated followers held back in deference as he stood smiling before Clytemnestra.

'I greet my husband, Agamemnon, victorious King of Mycenae,' Clytemnestra announced loudly, her hands raised in greeting. 'I, our court and all the people of Mycenae welcome you home! The sun has risen anew over this kingdom now you are with us!' Elevating were her words yet they arose from a seething pit of darkness.

Agamemnon took and kissed her hand, murmured close to her ear, 'Ten years we have been apart, yes, ten years, but oh, I find you beautiful as the day I left. There is much, so very, very much I have to tell you.' In lowering darkness he turned briefly to the waiting crowd and, illuminated by firebrands held aloft in the hands of courtiers, he raised his arms high with drawn sword in his right hand as a gesture of victory. 'Let the enemies of Mycenae know I am returned!' he declared. 'Let them tremble before my sword and my spear!' People cheered from rooftop and window. Replacing the sword in its scabbard, facing Clytemnestra once more and taking her by the arm he said, 'Let us go inside.'

With those about them standing back they entered the high-walled forecourt but Clytemnestra, aware of two females, now emerged from among Agamemnon's group and following close, glanced over her shoulder. She soon recognised her daughter, Chrysothemis, returned from Troy with her father. The other woman, plainly gowned, slim, dark-haired, brown-eyed and strikingly attractive, she did not recognise. They hesitated and Agamemnon said, 'The man Chrysothemis would have taken as husband died bravely before the walls of Troy. The other woman is Cassandra, a daughter of King Priam himself. She is credited with the power of prophesy though I look forward still to seeing it fulfilled.'

'How very interesting,' remarked Clytemnestra. She knew perfectly well the role the alluring Cassandra must have played in her husband's life since the fall of Troy. Followed by the two girls, they continued on past the musicians who had ceased playing and had stepped back to allow them by. On entering the megaron they halted before the great hearth where the fire blazed and flames danced high in greeting for the newly returned king. Agamemnon, noting the hall almost devoid of

71

courtiers and others, except for the two girls and a pair of male slaves, said again, 'Yes, there is so very much I have to tell you,' adding, 'and one thing in particular if you do not yet know of it. Shall we sit and take wine?'

'Yes, wine,' replied Clytemnestra. 'I'll call for wine at once but now is not the time for me to sit,' She squeezed his arm then turned to one of the slaves to whom she spoke in a low voice. As the youth hurried away she said to Agamemnon, 'I beg you to say nothing more for now. No, say nothing at all, I insist. I have cleared almost everyone from the megaron to avoid your being unduly pestered, a feast is being readied in the dining hall as we speak but you, my husband and our king, must not appear care worn before the people of our, of your court. You must shine out as the conquering hero you surely are.'

'Conquering hero, bah,' muttered Agamemnon. 'A bath, yes, and a decent meal is all I'd like to conquer just now.'

The slave reappeared and handed each a large, well-filled goblet. Chrysothemis and Cassandra stepped back to sit by the hearth, Chrysothemis looking on in silence, Cassandra wide-eyed and seeming agitated. Clytemnestra and Agamemnon drank with Agamemnon hardly aware of his own wine being strong and undiluted.

'I will shortly take care of the two girls,' she informed him, glancing aside at them, 'but you must first refresh yourself. A hot bath is being prepared in our old rooms and I have a good robe of your own made fresh and ready. You will sit before your courtiers with me at your side then we will hear in full everything you have to tell us.'

'Yes, but - .' he began.

'No, please!' insisted Clytemnestra, as they crossed the great hall to enter the torch-lit passage from where they would ascend to the floor above, 'I will hear nothing more for the time being! Nothing at all! I will accompany you to our chambers then I'll return soon after. Please, I *must* hurry to oversee our preparations.'

Agamemnon gazed into her eyes and smiled, 'Oh, very well, but you have to know and it will, I'm sure, make you very happy.'

His words were lost amid the turmoil of her own thoughts.

The royal bath chamber, next to the royal bedroom was, in the light of day, colourfully decorated about its walls with leaping blue dolphins and other gliding creatures of the sea. Now, with only moon and stars visible beyond the window, it was illuminated by wavering flames from a cluster of oil lamps placed upon a table to one side of the king's bath, with a small number of others grouped at the far side of the room. The marine frescoes, once so vivid, had darkened to more enigmatic, sweeping forms that vanished into encroaching shadow.

Arcas, a pale, balding and willowy slave of the palace had completed his task of preparing the king's needs. Water heated by brazier in the ante-room, had been discharged steaming from a valved pipe positioned above the richly decorated ceramic tub. Cotton towels hung ready and there too, for the

73

king's convenience, were set out soap, a bronze razor and a jar of perfumed olive oil with an ornate strigil should he require any of these.

Arcas turned to the window from where he could gaze out over the moonlit hills and into the night beyond. Far to the west, lay his home town of Pisa from where, before attaining manhood, he had been one of several seized and abducted into slavery by Agamemnon in that renowned warlord's early days of kingship; that very Agamemnon who had cut down his own ruler, Tantalus. Arcas' instructions from his mistress, Clytemnestra, not one to lightly forgive disobedience, had been quite clear, 'Prepare the bath then you must be gone from there before your lord arrives.'

Steeped now in silence, Arcas wondered if young females, slaves or otherwise, would be sent up in advance, ready to attend their master. Perhaps soon they would be heard approaching and that would serve as warning for Arcas himself to leave. On the other hand, Agamemnon's wife, on this most momentous of days, might consider only her own presence appropriate. In pensive mood he continued to stare through the window. Lifting his gaze to the sweep of stars he recalled his earlier years at Pisa in the time of King Tantalus and mused upon long ago days with his family and his friends, all of them now but memories. He could escape from Mycenae and return to Pisa, but to what. He had nothing with which to pay his way, the town, he was told, had never recovered from the destruction inflicted upon it by Agamemnon and should he be caught, torture or a cruel death would most likely be his lot. Here he at least occupied relatively comfortable and secure surroundings compared to many of his kind, and he had enough to eat, especially after banquet leftovers were made available to such lowly occupants of the palace as was he. He stood in contemplation for longer than he ought to have, wondering how his life might have fared had not Pisa fallen to the Mycenaeans.

There were sounds from beyond the bathroom. People were approaching up the stairs and along the corridor. The voice, surely, of Clytemnestra. The voice, surely, of Agamemnon. Heart pounding, Arcas started toward the bedroom door but it was too late to avoid being seen. He had disobeyed her strict order to be gone before the king appeared and was greatly afraid. He turned away from the door, glanced at the window but all it offered was a fall to his death. With panic seizing him Arcas stepped quickly to the ante-room and slipped through the curtain to where still glowed the brazier used to heat the king's bathwater. There he puff-puff-puffed out the few oil lamps still burning. He waited, in near darkness, trembling with fear and hoping the sway of the curtain would not be noticed when they entered the dimly illuminated bathroom. Would they hear his breathing? Would they hear his thumping heart? Should he be discovered he might be branded, mutilated or worse because that was what happened to slaves who transgressed. Arcas closed his eyes and held his breath. The door beyond the ante-room opened and there were still only the two voices when they crossed to enter the bathroom. He listened as Clytemnestra uttered words in a soft and reassuring manner but he could not hear what she said. When the outer door closed the ensuing silence told him Agamemnon was alone in the bathroom. His back pressed against the wall, his head held down, his mouth ajar, Arcas breathed slowly, deeply and listened. Sounds of splashing water reached his ear and he relaxed thinking that, surely, no one could have reason now to look inside the ante-room. It seemed an age had passed before he heard the door to the bathroom reopen. Next to Arcas there was a small gap between curtain and wall, and caution by now having wavered in favour of curiosity, he turned his head aside and found himself able to observe that part of the chamber where stood the bath.

In the dining hall below, where burning firebrands were spaced about weapon-decorated walls, the noble courtiers, men only, apart from those women appointed to serve their pleasures, had gathered chattering amidst the heavy tables where rested gilded goblets and amphorae of honeyed wine. Pipes awaited the breath of their owners to bring forth music and colourfully attired jesters practised their arts. At one side of the room braziers hissed and spat where joints of beef and pork were being slowly turned. Soon there would be brought in dishes containing olives, figs and other vegetables, but for now the people waited for Agamemnon and Clytemnestra to make their regal appearance. Only a few wondered at the absence of Aegisthus, the man whose name they had been forbidden to utter.

A raven-haired young woman in plain dark gown entered the hall and heads turned. Those who had accompanied the king knew this was Cassandra, daughter of the dead King Priam and a mistress of Agamemnon. She glanced about, her expression one of trepidation but most took little notice of her and resumed their conversations. She drew breath, appeared twice about to speak but no words emerged. She gasped aloud, lifted her arms, palms outward with splayed fingers and as voices lessened and heads turned once more she cried out, 'Hear me – you must hear me! Your king is to be murdered! They are going to kill Agamemnon!'

Silence followed then someone asked, 'Who is this?'

'She's Cassandra,' declared one, 'our lord's new plaything!'

Another called, 'Who let her in here?'

'Won't you listen!' insisted Cassandra, staring about in despair, hands shaking. 'Listen to me - they are going to murder Agamemnon!'

Someone called for the palace guard and two armed men entered.

'Get her out of here!' ordered one of the courtiers. The two seized loudly protesting Cassandra and dragged her from the hall.

On the floor above, Clytemnestra had entered the bathroom. In her arms she clutched a folded, richly pattered garment that she let fall open as she approached Agamemnon who now was clambering awkwardly from his bath to reach for his towel, his balance affected by the wine taken not so long before. Closer now and Clytemnestra's shadow loomed ever larger above and behind her – a billowing darkness.

'This is for you, my darling,' she announced, smiling broadly, though the smile on her lips was not in eyes that reflected fitful flames of the lamps. 'There is not enough time for oil; your people, my dearest one, are becoming impatient.'

Arcas held his breath as she stopped before Agamemnon who laid aside his towel, saying with a laugh, 'Good – that's very good,' and reached out to take the garment. Arcas saw the dagger glint in her right hand as she drew back her arm. He was tempted to call out, 'No – oh, no!' but mortal fear stifled his voice.

'And this,' she cried aloud, 'is for Iphigenia and a child unnamed!' With all her strength Clytemnestra plunged the knife deep into his body close to where his heart lay then wrenched free the blade of vengeance. Agamemnon gasped, his eyes staring into hers, a hand reaching out to touch her as he sank groaning to his knees and their remained. Clytemnestra stepped back from him and paused, the knife dripping blood, she and Agamemnon a grim tableau frozen in surreal moments. A shattering crash! The heavy door was heaved back against the wall and another figure burst into the room. Arcas gaped in horror as Aegisthus, a hatchet grasped in his hand, strode across, thrust Clytemnestra aside, swung the weapon high and struck the dying man's head, splitting his skull wide so that Agamemnon toppled over as a slaughtered beast. Blood spread about the tiled floor and as both moved back from their fallen victim Clytemnestra turned in rage upon Aegisthus. 'You - you dammed stupid fool!' she screamed swinging the dagger up as if to strike him in the throat as their shadows performed a death dance about the walls. 'Why did you do that? Why? He can only die once and - and look at it – look at the mess you've made of him!'

Aegisthus let the bloodied hatchet drop to the floor with an echoing clatter, gaped at Clytemnestra who raised the knife closer still, its blade touching his flesh as he spluttered, 'I had to make sh-shure didn't I. Yes, didn't I. For both of us I did!'

'You drunken bastard!' she exclaimed, backing from him. 'It's the wine isn't it – yes, you're out of your damned pathetic wits!'

Aegisthus continued to stare as if lost for words then blurted, 'What if he'd k-killed you instead – what then?'

Ignoring the question, Clytemnestra, stepped further away from Aegisthus, from their victim and the dark pool of blood, to ask, 'How do I explain his death after what you just did – tell me? No, that's too much to expect from you isn't it. So how are people to think it was a natural death? Yes, tell me!' She glanced about the room then at her husband's body, adding with newfound calm, 'We have to move with haste and discretion don't we, my darling. I'll find those three slaves whose tongues I had cut out because of their lying and I'll send them up here. If you can manage as much, watch over them and make sure they clean away this fucking mess you've made – everything! Then empty that bath, have them wrap his body and leave it in there. D'you understand what I'm saying – do you? We have somehow to disguise what you've done and let no one see my dear husband's face – for both our sakes!'

'Yes,' Aegisthus burbled, 'I understand.'

'Well I do hope so. And are those men of yours still in the city?'

'Y-yes, they are and I – I already have them lodged here in the palace. It was against your wishes, I know but for this day I thought it -.'

'So you disobeyed me there did you,' she cut in. 'I suppose that's just as well. Get them in here and when those three slaves are done have them taken outside the city wall and make certain they're dealt with. I want no one to find their bodies. Is that clear – is it?'

Aegisthus glanced aside at the dead Agamemnon and mumbled, 'Alright, yes, I'll see it's all done - all as you ask.'

'Now,' she informed him, 'I must soon go down to the dining hall.' On reaching the door Clytemnestra turned to say, 'And you'll need to change that gown of yours, and your sandals; even in this light I can see they're spattered all over with his blood. Do that before you show your face downstairs - no, better if you keep out of the way altogether for another day or two!'

Arcas, shaking uncontrollably, watched Aegisthus lean back against the wall with hands pressed to his face. By the time the three mute slaves arrived he had recovered his senses as well as his hatchet. Under his threatening gaze, they began their loathsome task, staring ahead with fixed expressions in that grotesque, shadow-haunted chamber of death. Arcas backed away from the curtain, not caring to witness more or further risk discovery. Eyes closed, he sat to rest against the wall, thankful at least in knowing the cold water supply and outlet for waste were both with the bath and no further demands upon his brazier would be made.

Pipe music played and members of the court, expecting Agamemnon must make his seemingly delayed appearance before too much longer, stood in idle conversation. Clytemnestra had made her way to the crowded dining hall but had paused in the outside passage before entering. She drew breath then moved into view, wringing her hands and shaking her head in despair, her face wet with tears in the lurid light of the torches. Conversation died. Silence closed about the room. She raised her hands, gazed across expectant faces, then began, 'I – I fear I have terrible news for you. Terrible, terrible news indeed.' She drew breath once more, placed hands to her face for some moments then continued, 'Your king, my dear husband, who only today returned to our city in triumph, the gods have taken from us.' Heads turned from one to the other. Silence prevailed as she continued, 'I went to attend him at his bath but – but as he arose he cried out and grasped at his chest, calling for me. I could do nothing. I – I could not reach him in time as he fell aside. If only I had been able to –. Please, there are others with him now so I must return. I am stricken with grief and I can say nothing more.' Clytemnestra pressed hands back to her face, turned away and retraced her steps to the floor above.

A lingering silence ensued as she left the hall. Courtiers and guests looked to where Clytemnestra had stood then at one another. A murmuring rippled through the hall. It welled into uproar then transformed into animated chatter as what they had just heard dawned upon them as the truth. Some recalled the words of Cassandra but confusion ruled the evening.

Clytemnestra did not return to the scene of murder but passing by the door to the royal suite she hesitated. There were indistinct sounds from within but only one voice, that of Aegisthus. She could not see into the bedroom but guessed his men must be waiting there in the main room until the bathroom beyond was cleaned; the final task her three mute slaves would perform.

***

Darkness had fallen when, in a secluded garden within the palace compound I sat with my older sister, Chrysothemis; both of us with goblet in hand, the slave dismissed. Here a small fountain played, the air was warm and perfumed by flowers and above us, amid a sea of stars, hung a three-quarter moon. Despite our being daughters of Agamemnon we had not been invited to attend the dining hall for reasons, you understand, of propriety. Orestes had chosen to occupy his seat in the megaron in case pressing matters had to be dealt with in our mother's absence but would attend the dining hall when our father appeared. Chrysothemis and I, of course, expected to join our father in private next morning or, if time permitted, later that night when the banqueting and other diversions were ended.

Chrysothemis, now nineteen years of age, had much to tell me but first spoke of the fleet delayed at Aulis by storms, of the prophet Calchas and his pronouncements then of poor Iphigenia. She clutched my hand while saying with tears in her eyes, "It was just dreadful, you know, utterly dreadful. Many years have passed by but still I ask, how could our own father do something like that – how could he?"

"Did anyone actually witness what happened in all that darkness and rain?" I asked.

"No, of course not, except for the priests who did it, but we heard her cry out and next morning anyone who wished to look could see her blood spilled all about the sacrificial altar of Artemis. Father told us all she had been buried soon after within the temple precincts. Our mother had fled and Iphigenia was gone from us – gone forever, I know it. Our father is a man without mercy and I hate him – yes, I do."

Her feelings about a man who treated the death of others lightly I understood well enough but about the fate of our missing sister I somehow was not convinced, though I wasn't quite sure why. Chrysothemis described the sea voyage and the discomforts it had caused her, the attacks upon and plundering of Troy's allies. I asked her about Achilles, the great hero, and she said, "Yes, a great hero he was and he made sure everyone knew it. Father was jealous and took away his mistress so Achilles withdrew his support, refused to fight the Trojans then threatened to take to his ships with all his men and go home. Our side soon began to get

83

the worst of things but father still wouldn't budge. Instead he offered me as compensation – yes me, just like that. Treated me as one of his chattels he did and if the great hero didn't want me than he'd offer you instead. It wasn't until Achilles' closest friend took his place to preserve our honour then got himself killed that Achilles changed his mind and waded back in."

"So how did you feel when Achilles was killed?" I asked.

"Tell you the truth, I really wanted him at first but seeing the way he behaved towards other people changed my mind. When that fancy Trojan they say caused all the trouble in the first place got him with an arrow I wasn't terribly bothered." After a while her voice faltered and she said, "Look, Electra, I - I'm sorry but if you don't mind I'll talk more with you tomorrow. For now I'm very tired and must take to my bed. A decent bed is what I have sorely missed and at long last one awaits me, next to your own rooms, I believe."

"Yes, you get some sleep then we'll talk again in the morning. Find Melia; she'll take you up and help you get ready. I'll stay here a while longer and finish my wine."

She kissed my cheek, arose and slipped away into the darkness. I raised my cup. I was possessed by the night and thinking upon all she had said. The garden and the night spoke only of peace and tranquillity, touched by the breath of benign spirits. It was quite magical and I had no desire to leave.

I was finishing my wine when beyond the fountain I saw something move, a shadow amidst shadows. A cat, a dog? No, the form was too large. Someone as yet undisclosed had entered the garden. I stood up, tempted at first to hurry back indoors but instead I drew my breath and called, "Who is there? Show yourself!"

Several heartbeats, mine that is, passed before the figure arose from obscurity and approached. I was certain it must be a man. It, he, hesitated, still far enough away for me not to regard him as an immediate threat. "Lady Electra," came his voice, subdued yet brimming with anguish. "Please, I am Arcas, a slave of the palace and I have witnessed – I have witnessed -. No, I hardly dare speak of it in case I am overheard, yet I must tell you."

"Step forward and explain yourself," I called, rising from my seat. "There is no one else with me." I knew of Arcas, he assisted with our supply of hot water, and although he had never been of direct service to me I was certain he meant no harm. He moved closer until fully visible, hands clasped together, eyes wide with fear as he fell to his knees before me. "Lady Electra, please, I beg of you – if I reveal what I have seen this night I beg of you to tell no one it was I who spoke of it or Lady Clytemnestra will surely have me put to death. B-but I have to speak with someone or it will eat away my soul."

I had to reassure him, I had to know what he meant so I returned to my seat. "Arcas, you can confide in me now and I promise in the name of Zeus that if you yourself have done no wrong I will *not* betray you."

85

For eternal moments he looked down, then raised his head and began, "They have slain your father, our king. They have slain Lord Agamemnon. I was there and I saw what happened; I saw it all. May the gods preserve me, I saw and I heard everything."

I continued to stare at the wretched man, wondering if I'd perhaps misheard him but of course I had not. I peered across the garden but could see no one else, though most was in shadow or utterly dark. "Arcas," I said, calmly, though I was stricken with alarm, "tell me all that you witnessed and how."

"I filled the king's bath with hot water by command of – of Lady Clytemnestra. I was to leave as soon as this was done but I lingered with my thoughts until it was too late. I heard footsteps approach. I was afraid and hid away in the room where the brazier stands."

Without my interrupting, Arcas recounted in a trembling voice, his fingers locked tightly together, all he had seen and I knew he had to be telling the truth for what, otherwise, was to be gained. When finished he once more lowered his head to await my response.

"You must return to the palace and carry on as before," I told him. "The people there must by now know of this and I will wait to hear what they've been told. You should leave me now and avoid being seen until you are summoned."

"I can no longer go about my tasks," he responded, rising awkwardly to his feet. "I fear they will see guilt in my eyes and know my thoughts."

I understood his deep distress and no longer could I insist upon his resuming a life of servitude in the palace. "Very well," I said, "then stay close to my rooms this evening until I've found somewhere you can hide for the rest of the night. You must leave Mycenae well before sunrise tomorrow. I will give you enough of value to help you in the outside world until you find other service. I will tell no one what I heard until you're safely gone but I'll not mention your name. After you leave here you must say nothing more to anyone."

"May the gods bless and protect you Lady Electra," he said, giving me grateful bow.

I watched him vanish against the blackness of the palace building and though I waited a while longer in silence my thoughts were in turmoil. When I decided it was time I hurried up rarely used, narrow back stairs, located a storage room where Arcas could hide, then returned to my chamber outside which he waited amid columned shadows. I gave him a measure of gold as promised - a generous measure, and indicated the room where he could pass the night in safety. I hoped he would be well away from the city by daylight, a free man, never to return.

Once alone I wondered how our mother would account for our father's death. I was to find out soon enough.

Chapter 4
The Fate of Orestes

I had left the garden to ascertain the mood within the palace. In the megaron it was understandably subdued. Courtiers, priests, elders and attendants stood in small groups, gathered mainly about the great hearth where the fire still burned. They discussed matters in muted voice. Mere slaves were not, of course, involved in their conversations but remained here and there awaiting summons. White-haired Leucon sat where he usually did, a few steps away from the unoccupied throne, but the lyre, resting on his knees and clutched to his chest, was silent. Orestes was also absent so, feeling that I ought not to ask anyone about anything, I left for a while to breath fresh air and to think.

I saw no one else, not Orestes, not even Melia, until re-entering the megaron a little later that evening. On the throne sat mother with a group of people gathered about her, including members of the palace guard. She wore a plain, dark gown of Egyptian cotton that had her breasts for once covered. In the lesser throne next to hers but speaking to no one sat Orestes, also in plain tunic but with sword as always on view at his side. I moved discreetly about the hall and in listening to the more open conversations of others, I learned what was claimed to have happened to father. There was no sign of Aegisthus so I assumed he and his accomplices might be dealing with the three slaves they intended to slaughter, unless they had already done so. Perhaps the misery those three men endured was best ended by death. Orestes at last spotted me, left his seat and walked across to where I stood.

"Well what d'you think of all this?" he asked. "Just back from laying waste to Troy then the old man goes and dies getting out of his bath. Maybe ten years of plundering and warfare were too much for him."

"We have to talk somewhere in complete privacy," I said.

"Why d'we need to do that? I can't get away yet; I'm giving our dear mother my support at present for what it's worth, and Aegisthus can't take the seat while I'm sitting on it."

"I understand what you're saying, Orestes, but if not now then in my rooms and sooner the better. We really *must* talk and it *has* to be in secret. I will wait."

He nodded and started back across the hall. At that point, to my right, I saw Aegisthus enter from a side corridor. He paused by a column and stared hard at Orestes as my brother returned to the seat next to mother. I was quite certain it was to there Aegisthus intended to take himself but for now he was thwarted. Mother noticed him also and appeared most displeased over his presence. Aegisthus' expression was darker still as he turned and strode out. Others stopped to discuss matters with me, including Chrysothemis, to ask what I thought of what our mother had told them and convinced, of course, that it was perfectly true. Had my sister known what I had been told I believe she would have fled straight to her rooms and next day looked for a party going to Corinth. The crowds in the megaron were thinning out as people returned to the dining area. There was, after all, food still laid out and waiting but I decided I would go back to my rooms and await Orestes even though it might be some time before he was able to join me. About to leave I noticed in the shadows of a colonnade to my left another figure in a dark gown standing alone, her face part concealed by a cowl. Cassandra. I made my way over to her, passing the throne where mother was still engaged in conversation and Orestes patiently listening. The girl, a dark-eyed beauty little older than myself, stared at me with uncertain gaze as I introduced myself. "I am Electra, a daughter of Agamemnon and Clytemnestra. You find yourself abandoned in a strange land with nowhere to go. I would like to help you."

She continued to stare at me then said, "Agamemnon was murdered. I tried to warn them but just as in Troy no one would believe me. No one ever does; not until it's too late."

"I know you spoke out in the dining hall and I – I heard how they rebuked you. Let us sit and talk at the far side of the hearth where we'll not be overheard but will be in view of my brother. Later I'll find you a room for the night with one of our girls, or better still you must share with me; I'm sure I have all you may need." Hers was a smile of resignation as we stepped across to the circular hearth. "Will you take wine?" I asked as we sat.

"No," she replied, "I need nothing. Nothing at all."

"Cassandra, you spoke the truth. I know what happened to my father. I know he was murdered and I know who did it."

"Yes, you do, don't you. You know everything."

"You were not believed because – because how could anyone be expected to believe he would be murdered on the day of his return after ten years absence at Troy?"

"If you think upon your own question," she answered, letting the cowl slip from her head, "you will surely know why, but I will understand if you don't believe that either."

"But why will no one accept what you foresee if what you tell has in the past proven true?" In her dark pool eyes I saw another world; one beyond my understanding but one of great sadness also as she answered my question.

"Not so long ago, when I was but fifteen years old I had two dreams - dreams unlike anything else before or since. In the first of these Apollo came to me and asked for my hand in marriage. If I agreed to this he would bestow upon me the power of prophesy. I did agree and at first it seemed his promise was true even though it had been no more than a dream. I was confused but in small matters I practised those powers and they worked. Yes it – it was really so, and some began to consult me though others made out the results of my predictions were no more than chance. For a time I half believed that myself." She looked aside, raised a hand to wipe tears from her eyes then continued. "Soon after this I fell in love with another man, a real man, a man of flesh and blood, and when Apollo next appeared to me and asked that I comply with my promise I rejected him for the mortal man. As punishment he laid a curse upon me, a curse that meant I would never again be believed even if my prophesies were true, which he determined they always would to be."

"But these *were* only dreams," I assured her. "How can they be true in real life?"

"But the gods *do* visit us in our dreams do they not and I know only too well how that curse afflicts me. In Troy I knew the Greeks were to bring defeat upon us but I was scorned or simply ignored. In those final days, when they constructed that monstrosity in the form of a wooden horse and left it outside the city gate, I knew there were men inside it. I warned and begged my father not to have his men drag it within the city wall. I insisted they should break up or burn the thing but they regarded it as an offering willed by the gods themselves. Yes, they dismissed my words and now most of them, including my father, are dead."

"And what now are your thoughts?" I asked her.

"The House of Atreus is still with you; all the hate and violence never died but is handed down to all who succeeded that terrible man. Hatred and vengeance live in the very walls as a seeping poison. They wait to emerge from the dark corners, from the secret depths of this place and will never rest until – well, never mind."

This was hardly a prediction since I already knew it, so I asked her, "Can you tell me then, what lies ahead for you, for me and for my brother?"

Cassandra lowered her head and raven hair fell across her eyes as she whispered, "No, I can say nothing more – there is no point in doing so. I wish only to rest."

I felt so very sorry for her but what, just then, could I do? Yet I was determined to have her as my friend and to help her in any way possible. As we stood to leave I noticed Orestes watching us with a broad grin. Mother was watching us also, but her expression was fixed and unsmiling. Cassandra looked straight ahead and followed me up to my rooms but she seemed reluctant to engage in further conversation, so we sat side by side by my window gazing out to the stars. Behind us, opposite the window, a cluster of oil lamps burned. At last there were footsteps outside, a tapping on my door that opened to reveal Orestes. He entered, smiled at me then for several moments he gazed admiringly at Cassandra. Her lips moving as though with silent words, she paused to smile at him as if she knew him well. I poured wine for Orestes and myself then had him sit close by us. We each tasted our wine then I said, "Orestes, our father did not suffer a failure of his heart or anything of the kind. He was murdered."

Orestes gulped and coughed, "M-murdered?"

"Yes, and the man who witnessed everything that happened, a slave of the palace, came to me for help because he needed to tell what he'd seen and could not disguise his fear of being recognised because of it. He heard also what was said, he described every detail and I know he spoke the truth. I gave him gold and some items of value and he will soon flee the city."

Orestes stared at Cassandra. "By the gods I was told you warned everyone he was to be murdered so you, Electra, with your witness, you must know who did this."

"Yes I do - it was our own mother and Aegisthus. She always hated father because of Iphigenia; because he sacrificed his own daughter – our sister, on the altar of Artemis."

"That is so," breathed Cassandra. "It is a hate that burned long and deep within her, a brooding, burning vengeance concealed within a bosom of ice."

Orestes stared at us and doubt slipped from him as chaff in a breeze as he said, "Very well, explain to me exactly what this man of yours witnessed."

I repeated as closely as I could all that Arcas had told me then added, "I wonder will anyone be allowed to look closely upon father's body. Surely not; such a wound as that inflicted by Aegisthus' hatchet would give the lie to our dear mother's claims."

"We'll have to see what happens when they bury him won't we," said Orestes, "and that can't be far away." Orestes and I agreed, for the time being, not to disclose to anyone else what we knew had really happened to our father. But what of Cassandra? I had her remain with me that night but few words passed between us before it was time to sleep. It seemed to me that, in her mind, she had already passed into another world. She stayed by my side much of the following day when we were joined by Chrysothemis who, of course, still knew nothing of the murder. Late in the afternoon Cassandra informed me that mother had asked to speak with her. She failed to reappear that evening, but my time was occupied in discussing our affairs with Orestes and our sister who, on learning the truth of our father's death, wished only to be far away from Mycenae. I concluded other accommodation had been found for Cassandra. Next day saw the court busied with preparations for father's funeral so Chrysothemis and I joined a group of my friends in one of our favourite spots, the garden where I had been approached by Arcas that fateful evening. I had hoped Cassandra would join us there but when she did not, I assumed she had preferred to be alone.

***

Two days after the murder, in early morning sunlight, a measured beat of drums announced the approach of the procession as it descended the stone ramp leading from the palace buildings toward the Lion Gate. Before reaching the gate it would bear left and enter the stone circle that had been Mycenae's burial place allocated generations ago to the great and good. More recent generations of those who ruled had been consigned to the great tholos tombs built into hillsides outside the city but this ancient, sacred and revered site was considered more appropriate for Mycenae's greatest of heroes. Here a deep and spacious shaft had been prepared and valuable items and weapons readied for internment with Agamemnon.

Led by an austerely robed Clytemnestra and Orestes in plain tunic, the bier was carried by six of those warriors who had accompanied their king to Troy, bronze-clad with black horsehair plumes swaying above sun-glinting helmets as they walked with slow and dignified steps to the beat of the drum. Already gathered about the grave were the nobles, priests and elders of Mycenae. The many onlookers who jostled together on the city wall, behind parapets or pressed together at windows had a fine view of the bier and saw how their dead lord was attired in his robes of kingship. They observed also how his face was covered entirely by a close-fitting mask of beaten gold. That was the face of Agamemnon people saw. It was the face they had to see. As the funeral party approached the open grave, the drumming ceased, the onlookers quietened and the priests began their chants and incantations. This continued while the body was lowered slowly into final darkness together with those possessions allocated to it. Those observing close enough watched jewelry, items of gold, silver, amethyst and amber, vessels of precious metals, faience and alabaster, objects of carved ivory and numerous weapons arranged around the floor of the tomb. Libations of milk, honey, water and wine, were poured into the grave as it was filled with earth, as was the blood of a ritually sacrificed sheep and a pig. Slaves, under the watchful eyes of accompanying guards, continued filling the shaft to the slow beat of the drums.

From the city wall, accompanied by a member of the palace guard, Electra and Chrysothemis watched, hearing the rise and fall of voices, seeing how people pointed and chattered. Electra strained to observe Aegisthus but could see nothing of him. Cassandra she did not expect to see. Why, she thought, would a daughter of Priam wish to witness, even in death, the man who had destroyed her home, her father and so many of those she cherished? The sun was approaching its zenith and the day pleasantly warm when the grave shaft was filled, the earth beaten and a stela erected. With the ceremony ended the crowds began to diminish. Electra and her sister took the easiest way back to the palace, following the city wall until they reached descending steps. Others, also, were returning to the cooler interior of the buildings. Electra looked about for Cassandra in the megaron. She searched in other rooms and in the small, enclosed gardens accessible only from the palace, then in her own suite on the floor above. Cassandra was nowhere to be seen. She returned with ominous feelings to the megaron where Clytemnestra had reoccupied her throne with Orestes sitting close by.

***

I searched again later, asking other people around the court if anyone had seen Cassandra. None had. By sunset I took my last meal of the day with Chrysothemis and some of my court friends then we sat about the table in conversation with me all the time hoping Cassandra would reappear. I knew somehow, I knew deep down, she would not. A fear was stirring within me; loose threads weaving together a dark curtain that concealed a despicable truth.

The following morning I entered the megaron to see mother steeped in conversation with two of her courtiers while Leucon played gentle notes. I made straight for her. Perhaps it was the expression on my face that had her dismiss those in discussion with her but as I approached, that is what she did. To my great disappointment there was no sign of Orestes.

"Where is Cassandra?" I demanded aloud. Leucon stopped playing.

She stared at me for some moments then replied, "Why are you asking me; I'm not responsible for her. Maybe she's left the city."

"Left the city - really! And where d'you think she'd go – back to Troy?" She continued to stare at me and I said, "Then perhaps we should ask that poor substitute you have for a husband."

Hands gripping hard on the sides of her seat she looked ready to rise in anger to confront me. Poor old Leucon raised himself up and tottered away gripping his precious lyre. "I'll have you know," she insisted, "that whatever you think of the man, he has lifted a great burden from my shoulders and well you know it." She relaxed somewhat then continued with news that shocked me. "And as you'd find out sooner or later I'll tell you right now – I have appointed Aegisthus head of our palace guard."

"Head of -!" I gasped.

"Head of our palace guard," she repeated, "though he can make no real decisions without my consent. It is a responsibility needing someone with more commitment than I am able give. He will have enemies, I know that well enough so his own men will serve as his personal protection."

"Well he's hardly the man Periphas was, is he mother. You remember Periphas don't you – the man found murdered outside the city wall? He was in and out of your bed often enough!"

"You will regret speaking to me like that!" she exclaimed, leaping to her feet.

At that point Aegisthus appeared at the far end of the megaron, attired in the manner of a court noble. On seeing him make his way over to us, mother's expression of anger dissolved into a broad smile and she lowered herself back into the comfort of her throne. "Electra would like to know where that Trojan woman Cassandra's got to," she said, looking at him with an expression of innocence. "Have you seen her or d'you know where she is?"

Aegisthus glanced from her to me then back again without expression, shrugged and answered, "How would I know?" He then called for wine.

"Yes, how would you," I muttered. As I turned to leave, Aegisthus was seating himself beside her. I decided to go and find Orestes, thinking he might be busy outside the city wall leaning how best to kill people. I was crossing the anteroom outside the megaron when he entered from the courtyard outside, his tunic soiled, his sword swinging at his side.

"Found your friend yet?" he asked. "Wouldn't mind finding her myself."

"We're not going to find her," I said. "I don't think we or anyone else are ever going to and even if we did, Orestes, she'd be too old for you."

He took a deep breath, looked past me toward the great hall and replied, "Are you saying they've somehow got rid of her? You are, aren't you."

"That bitch of a woman we call our mother and the creature she shares her bed with murdered our father so I don't suppose they'd want his mistress from Troy getting under their feet. If I'm right the poor girl must have seen her own death coming but could tell no one, not even me, for even I might not have believed her. What's more, Aegisthus is back in your seat next to mother and she's appointed him head of the palace guard."

"Yes, I was told that by one of the men – and in my place is he!" With that Orestes' hand fell to his sword hilt and he started forward.

"No!" I exclaimed, seizing his arm. "No, it's too dangerous. He'll be armed, he's more experience than you and there are men he can call upon quickly for help; they're already here in the palace."

Orestes stepped back, saying, "Yes, I - look, let's get out of here for a while; there's something else you ought to know." We left the building, stepped into sunlight, found a low stone wall to sit upon and Orestes said, "One of the men also thinks he's made those five oafs his personal bodyguard. Our mother never told *me* about that."

"Yes, that's exactly what I'm saying; she informed me of it just before I came looking for you. She didn't even want them in the city until now and I'm sure they'll be at his beckoning somewhere close to the megaron or her rooms. She must have been in full agreement over this unless he's somehow coerced her. So if Aegisthus holds that much power and rules as mother's consort, as it seems he now does, you may be in great danger."

"Are you saying our own mother would have *me* done away as well?"

"No, not her, but if Aegisthus gains enough power in Mycenae at her expense, then -."

"Then I have to watch my back, don't I."

"Yes, he'll expect you to be plotting against him and I'm sure that's what you intend. And there's something else; if she has a child by Aegisthus and it's a boy, they'll regard him as next in line to the throne and your position will be far worse than it is now."

Orestes was silent for a time then breathed, "Er, yes, I see what you mean."

"Look, Orestes, you might think you're a grown man but you're still only sixteen. Get away from Mycenae for a while with your friend, Pylades. Maybe he'll go with you since you both get on so well together. Take whatever items of value you need. I'll give you gold pieces as well, and go to Delphi; the two of you could do that. Consult the oracle or one of the priests then maybe go on to Sparta where I'm sure Menelaus will welcome you. Please, do this for my sake as well as your own."

"I er, I'll need to think hard about that," he answered, "but maybe I will talk to Pylades."

We agreed to meet again later the following day and I hoped by then my brother might have reached a decision of sorts. Meanwhile I located Chrysothemis chatting with some friends and persuaded her to join me in the privacy of my own rooms with a welcoming dispensation of honeyed wine. Once the slave had gone I felt I had to tell her all. I explained most of what I had learned including, of course, the details of our father's murder. She was shocked and naturally upset but other matters were of only passing importance since she had less interest by far than I did in palace affairs. One of her main concerns, now the contingents had returned from Troy, had been the appearance of suitors. Despite the reputation long since acquired by the House of Atreus, the wealth of Mycenae and its court were very much an attractive prospect for alliance.

"They'll be wanting to set eyes on you as well," Chrysothemis remarked at one point, "and it may be a chance for you to get out of here."

"I'm not interested in eyes being set on me at present," I informed her, "but I definitely *am* worried about Orestes."

"Better if he keeps his head down, don't you think?"

"That wouldn't be at all like our brother but the way things are going here he may be lucky to keep his head at all unless he leaves Mycenae."

"No, Electra, don't say that! They surely wouldn't -."

"Oh, wouldn't they! With Aegisthus in direct charge of those ruffians and mother letting him have more of his own way, we don't know what might happen – especially when the wine takes him over."

"I – I don't know what to think," she sighed, sipping more wine then placing aside her goblet. "Maybe we both should talk to Orestes and get him to exercise more care. It's his age you know, but perhaps he'll see sense if we try."

"Perhaps," I sighed.

***

Early next morning my brother joined me to sit in the same secluded garden as I had before. The air was delightfully cool and I hoped its freshness might help concentrate his thoughts.

"I chatted to Pylades," Orestes informed me. "He's willing to visit Delphi but not so sure about staying away for too long even though he has little to do with the court. My concern is for you and our sister. I can't turn my back on you both so I say we wait a while; I have a good relationship with our palace guard since I've spent enough of my time with them. They treat me as one of their own so I see no problems there."

"If you insist, but Orestes, what Arcas described of our father's murder and what now I'm certain has happened to Cassandra is burning inside me. I have to make known my feelings to our mother sooner or later or I'll be consumed with madness. Stay out of their sight, Orestes, please. Just stay *out* of their sight!"

***

It was later that same day when I decided to confront her. I had put back a lot of wine; enough so I thought, to fortify myself - more wine than I

103

should have. I found mother sitting alone in the megaron. I say alone because Aegisthus was not present though a small number of courtiers and other people were standing about in conversation.

"How great a say in our affairs are you going to allow that man," I asked her, "or is it no longer your decision? Is he to plan all our futures from your bed?"

She stared at me coldly then responded, "I've told you before why I need him so what is the point in your making a fool of yourself and trying to embarrass me in front of others by keeping on and on about it? And *my* private life is hardly any of *your* business! From the way you carry on perhaps it's a man *you* need in *your* life - you're certainly old enough. Yes, that's what it is; you're becoming frustrated."

Perhaps I did want a man, yes it *was* what I wanted - what I needed, but as things were I regarded that as impossible. Our raised voices had not until then attracted the attention of others but then, having relinquished what remained of my self-control I declared, "Aegisthus doesn't think much of me, we both know that, and I fear I might wake up one morning and find Orestes no longer with us, like it was with Cassandra!" She appeared visibly shocked as I added, "And I know *exactly* how our father died!" She glared hard, hands clutching at the fabric of her gown and appeared about to rise from her throne. I knew there and then I should not have said what I had but it was as if some demon within was compelling me on as I continued, "It was revealed to me that very same evening. It was all witnessed by a slave hiding in the ante-room where the braziers stand!" By now all other conversation had ceased and people had turned to look and listen. "The man described how you stabbed father with a knife concealed in the gown you offered him as he climbed from his bath and how your dear, sweet Aegisthus rushed in with an axe to finish the job in case father was still not dead! Isn't that right, mother! Isn't it!"

"Th-that's a preposterous lie and you know it!" she cried, rising from her throne. "Call for that man to come here and repeat what you claim he told you. Get him before me right now!"

"No, mother, his life wouldn't be worth a shattered pot and you know it! But don't worry because he'll by this time be safely away from the city." She stared about the megaron, mouth ajar, then turned to address me once more but by then I was hurrying around the great hearth and on my way out. Once in the open air I stood shaking, looking desperately about to see if Orestes was anywhere in sight. I had to warn him over what I had so very foolishly revealed. I could see no sign of him in his usual spot outside the city wall so I returned and made my way past the megaron up to his private chamber. As I approached his door it opened and a fair-haired young girl emerged, bare foot and busily adjusting her fancy cotton gown. She hurried by to the stairs, grinning sheepishly as she passed me by then disappeared from view. She was certainly not a slave but who she was I had no idea and was of no mind to ask as I stood in his doorway.

"We need to talk some more," I said, once inside. He straightened the woollen cover on his dishevelled bed and gestured for me to sit close by. I seldom visited his room for it possessed few of the comforts to be found in my own, though like most members of our immediate family he did have his own bath. "I confronted our mother in the megaron," I informed him. "I should never have done it, I realise that, at least not until you and I had discussed it further, but I told her what we know. Standing before her, I - I couldn't help it."

"Er, yes," he breathed, tightening the belt of his tunic, "maybe that wasn't a good idea but I wouldn't have minded seeing her face."

"You know what will happen next, don't you – she'll be discussing it with *him* and they'll see you above all as liable to conspire against them with some of father's old companions in the palace guard or beyond. I'm sorry, Orestes, I truly am but I don't know how long we, or I, could have kept up the pretence anyway."

"Quite, so maybe your idea of my drifting off for a while to Delphi was no bad thing. I'll talk about it again with Pylades."

"Make it sooner rather than later," I said, kissing him on the cheek before hurrying off to my own den of comfort where I had much soul-searching to do. "Poor, dear Cassandra," I whispered when seated by my window, "What have they done to you?"

***

The evening was drawing to a close with stars visible through the high windows of the great hall.

Only firebrands relieved total darkness where a smouldering fire in the circular hearth spat and settled. Soon, apart from Clytemnestra, the great hall would be deserted with all but one of the slaves dismissed. Yet there remained unseen one other. Leucon had played his last notes a while earlier but did not consider it proper to leave the hall unless permitted to do so. The old man was tired and, clutching his lyre, had shuffled aside to rest for a while out of sight in the dark area behind a column close to the throne. The seat next to the throne was as yet unoccupied. Soon Leucon was sleeping soundly.

Footsteps approached yet still Leucon slept and continued to do so even as Aegisthus greeted Clytemnestra and took his place beside her. Only when Aegisthus called aloud for wine did Leucon stir, opening his eyes, raising his head and for a time, wondering where he was or why. He heard Aegisthus dismiss the slave and heard him ask Clytemnestra, 'Do we discuss things upstairs or do we stay here in the hall?'

'We can stay where we are for now,' she replied. 'There's no one to hear us; I think that's obvious enough.'

Leucon, now fully awake, eased himself higher against the column, realised Clytemnestra and Aegisthus were unaware of his being close by and for a moment wondered if he ought to reveal his presence. Then, no, he would appear foolish and perhaps end up in disgrace. Clytemnestra and Aegisthus must soon, he considered, take to their beds, or both to hers, as well established gossip had

107

verified, so discretion would be Leucon's choice and he would try to resume sleeping.

'We have a problem, don't we,' said Aegisthus. 'I heard what that daughter of yours came out with in front of you and others down here. How could anyone have -.'

'Three problems, actually, darling,' she cut in, 'Orestes and Chrysothemis will by now have the whole story from Electra and they'll believe it even if other people don't.'

'Or you – we, *hope* other people don't.'

'Quite, I think everyone who heard it was shaken by what she said but I managed to convince them that the outburst was a result of her mind being poisoned by that Trojan girl and a surfeit of wine. I've made it clear also that she's been unwell of late and prone to distressing nightmares, which is why few people have noticed her around. I do, however, see more trouble coming our way.'

'And so do I,' said Aegisthus, 'so how d'you propose we deal with the situation, after all, they're your children? Orestes has plenty of friends in the palace guard and he'll be thinking already how to set himself against us both. I suspect you being his mother won't matter in the least and he'll see me as dead already.'

'Yes, my own son – what *are* we to do.'

'You know as well as I,' replied Aegisthus, 'there's only one thing we can do is there not.'

'We? No, I cannot be involved in the killing of my own son, though I suspect he'd shed no tears if I were dead and gone tomorrow. Apart from anything else the gods would see it as the greatest of sins and should the truth come out the whole city as well as the palace guard would quickly turn against me – against us.'

'Then you're saying it's left to me alone are you not.'

'Perhaps I am. You'd murder your own mother after a few drinks wouldn't you, dear, and damn the consequences - unless you've had her done away with already.'

'I have those men of my own, as you know, and they have little contact with others here. An accident, perhaps. No one would know what happened. Sooner the better, I say.'

'Yes, you would, wouldn't you,' breathed Clytemnestra. 'Those men of yours - yes, very convenient aren't they, and it seems we have no choice though this could damage some of our alliances, particularly that with Sparta. Menelaus regards his brother's children rather highly.'

'So what about those two girls?'

Clytemnestra stared across to the hearth before replying. 'Chrysothemis is taken up more with the prospect of suitors now there are so many worthies back from Troy but she otherwise keeps out of palace affairs. Electra is consumed by a desire for vengeance but I'll not have her harmed. I lost my firstborn at Pisa and then Iphigenia before she'd reached womanhood, both at the hand of my darling husband. We'll need to keep a close eye on Electra until such time she begins to see reason. I'll talk to her; I will explain why Agamemnon *had* to die. Perhaps then -.'

Leucon breathed slowly and quietly, fearful in case the lyre slipped against something hard, fearful in case he should accidently pluck one of the strings. The words passing between those close above were intended for no one. For Leucon, if discovered, they would prove a death sentence.

They drank and finished their wine, saying little else, then placed their goblets onto the floor; one of them well within an arm's reach of Leucon who closed his eyes and feigned sleep in case his presence should at last be revealed. He watched two pairs of feet step very close to where he lay and he held his breath as Clytemnestra and Aegisthus proceeded from sight across the megaron. For some time he listened hard but dared not stir though his limbs ached. Then a hiss from the dying fire in the hearth somehow assured him that no one else was present as, clutching his lyre, he emerged from the space by the column and with head lowered, made his cautious, stooping way in near darkness from the great hall.

***

I had arisen from an uneasy night's sleep and stepped through to my main room. There was but a merest hint of dawn beyond my window when I heard the voice. It sounded hardly more than a whisper but it spoke my name from beyond the outer door where lay the corridor. I listened for some moments then hurried back into the bedroom, pulled on my gown and returned to face the door. Again the voice and I called, "Who's there?"

"It is I, Leucon," came the barely audible reply.

The swaying flame of the single lamp I held in my hand was barely enough to illuminate his face as I opened the door. "Leucon," I asked, "what brings you here and why so early?"

I had never before seen him this far from the megaron yet he obviously knew where to find me. "Lady Electra," he began, clutching his lyre and slightly out of breath through climbing the stairs from the floor below, "I - I must speak with you. I have lain awake throughout the night thinking what I have to do and the only persons I can confide in is yourself or your brother. I hear from gossip that the young master is sometimes with the company of another at night and I'd dare not risk being seen in close conversation with him during the day or any time if in the megaron."

"Come inside," I said. His eyes were wide with apprehension as I closed the door and gestured for him to rest by me near to the window. This he was reluctant to do, so I had him sit away from the window where he laid aside his lyre. "Leucon, you appear greatly troubled. What has happened?"

"When most people had left the megaron," he began in a low voice, "I went to rest in the space behind that column closest to the throne of Lady Clytemnestra and there I fell asleep unseen. I awoke to overhear her conversation with the man she has taken as her consort and all the time they were unaware of my presence. Had they known I was there and able to hear what was said, Aegisthus would have driven his sword into me there and then – I know he would."

"Will you take wine to help calm your thoughts?" I asked.

"No, if you please, I will not, I wish only to say what I have to say then return to where I may rest alone."

I sat by my loom and asked him to continue.

"Lady Electra, he, that man of hers, wishes to see your brother dead. He will have those who came to Mycenae with him do the deed." He continued on, relating all he had heard in detail, to me alone, as with the account given by Arcas of my father's murder. His words chilled me through. It was obvious Orestes was in great danger and had to be warned at once. When Leucon had finished, as morning light had banished the stars beyond my window, I asked him, "Do you wish to hide for a time or leave Mycenae? I will help you either way."

"Hide – leave Mycenae! No, I'll do neither, I'm far too old for that. I'll carry on as I was - as I have all these years in this - this blighted House of Atreus. Now I've told you what I heard, I have less fear of them but I'll pray the gods protect your brother." He arose, collected up his lyre, stepped over to the door then turned to add, "I will now take my sleep and let them wonder at my absence. And when I return to the megaron I'll sing aloud in praise of Agamemnon and his deeds at Troy and hope my words torment them both even should they guess why I'm doing it."

"Take good care, Leucon," I breathed. "Don't make them suspicious."

It seemed I was fated to hear before all others the evil doings of my mother and her ill-chosen consort. I pulled on a heavier gown. It was my intention to speak with Orestes as soon as I could find him but on leaving my chamber I encountered Melia in the passage on her way to attend to my bathing. "Have you seen my brother?" I asked. The girl looked at me with guilt clouding her face but seemed reluctant to speak.

"Well answer me!" I insisted, but I had already drawn my own conclusions when she wrung her hands together and gazed down at the stone floor. "I really don't care if you've spent this last or any other night with Orestes," I assured her, "all I want to know is where he is right now."

"W-we took food and drink together while it was still dark," she replied, raising her head to look directly at me. "I know by now he will have left to join his men outside the city wall."

I forced a smile, squeezed her arm to allay any fear of reprimand she might have, but still I needed to enter his room. It was, as Melia had me thinking, unoccupied, so I carried on to the chamber allocated to Chrysothemis only to find her door was bolted on the inside. I concluded she must still be asleep and so I hurried to the stairs. I first entered the dining hall where many were taking their first meal of the day but Orestes, unsurprisingly, was nowhere in sight and none of the girls I often chatted with claimed to have seen him that morning. On passing through the megaron I noted mother watching me from her throne but Aegisthus was not there. Neither was Leucon, though he was occasionally not seen until later in the day. I experienced both anger and fear, wondering if Aegisthus' men had already found my brother then I continued on to exit the palace. I had set off along the great ramp for once unaccompanied, hesitating to see mourners still gathered about my father's grave before I made my way out beneath the Lion Gate. Traders and others passing by looked aside, wondering no doubt why anyone in court dress should be outside the city unaccompanied even by slaves. Court dress it may have been, yes, but not just then as revealing above the waist as that usually worn by my mother. I was much relieved on seeing Orestes with his friend Pylades and his warrior group in their usual place and I approached to see him let loose an arrow that penetrated the dead pig, one of their customary targets. He spotted me and strode over, shaking his bow in the air and informing me with a smile, "See that did you? I skewered Aegisthus three times already and again just now with my fourth shot! So what brings you out here this early in the morning on your own?"

As we faced one another I replied, "We have to talk before you return to the city."

"Oh, this *does* sound important," he grinned.

"It *is* important and it's not funny; the real Aegisthus is planning to skewer *you*."

"What," he laughed, patting his sword hilt, "then I'll catch *him* out first!"

"No, you have to listen to *me* first. Where can we sit for a while out here?"

"Well there's a handy slab of rock over there," he replied, pointing to his right. "You'll have to do without cushions, though."

"Yes, Orestes, I'll do without cushions." We stepped across to sit in the innocence of morning sunlight with insects buzzing lazily about and there, as he stared quizzically at me, I revealed to him the ominous information related by Leucon.

"Then I have to stop him, don't I," declared Orestes when I had finished my account.

"Look," I responded, "it's not just Aegisthus; he's got those five armed men of his somewhere in the palace ready to be called upon. You're only sixteen and they're probably hardened killers. Just lately I've seen one or two of them outside the megaron talking to Aegisthus but I'm sure the others are never far away."

"And our dear mother didn't even want them in the city to start with, did she."

"No, she didn't but Aegisthus is having ever more of his own way and she doesn't appear to care too much."

"D'you think he has any real feelings for our loving mother?" Orestes asked.

"I didn't think so to begin with but now I'm not sure. He came here intending to use her, a mere woman, as a way of gaining authority but she's won him over in other ways, as we know, and now he wants the best of both worlds. But never mind that. Orestes, do as I have already asked you; do it for my sake as well as your own and leave Mycenae for a while – Sparta, maybe. Stay away until you're a bit older and maybe have gathered outside support, but keep in touch with me. Talk to Pylades today and see if he'll join you, then tonight you must stay in my room in case Aegisthus calls on those men of

115

his. I will add small items of my own, gold and silver, to whatever you have so before dawn tomorrow you can leave the city in safety."

"I don't like this," he declared. "I'd be running away and leaving you to their mercy. No, I can't do that."

"Orestes, listen to me! I say again, it is for *my* sake as well as yours. I'm begging you!"

"And what about our sister?"

"Chrysothemis, as we're both aware, prefers a quiet life and doesn't want to be involved in any of this. All she's concerned about now she's back in Mycenae is meeting the right man who will get her well away from here and I can't say I blame her."

"Nor me," he shrugged. "But you'll have suitors of your own – men hoping to renew or strengthen their alliance with Mycenae and it'll also be what our mother wants."

"She can want whatever she likes but I doubt if she, or Aegisthus, will have me telling all that I know of them and creating mistrust with potential allies."

"What d'you think she'll do as far as you're concerned?" he asked.

"I wouldn't like to say but I'm sure I'll not be in the kind of danger you are. I'd better return now but join me this evening, please."

For much of that day Orestes continued to indulge in his combat games with those men he could trust. I returned to the palace, avoided the megaron, took food and wine with two of my friends then went to my rooms. There I occupied myself at my loom, more in thinking over what was happening than in weaving though across the loom lay a half completed shawl.

Someone tapping on my door had me rise quickly and ask a second time that day, "Who is there?"

"It is I, Melia," came her voice. When I opened the door she asked me, sheepishly, "Is there anything you wish for, Lady Electra – anything at all?"

I thought for some moments then replied with a smile, "I had no time to bathe earlier – perhaps now?" I hoped, with her attentive company, I might forget our troubles for at least a part of that morning.

***

I stayed away from the megaron throughout that afternoon strolling with friends, all of us plainly dressed, through the busy market then up to the city wall where, in a pleasant breeze, we watched the blazing glow of sunset. I of course disclosed nothing of what had happened earlier in the day.

Well after sunset, as I had asked, Orestes joined me in private, a leather satchel hung over his shoulder, his sword as always at his side and now with a short spear in his hand. He unburdened himself of these possessions and we took wine and food I had ordered a short time before.

"I hope no one saw you coming here," I said.

"No," he assured me, "I checked the corridors and stairs first. There were so few torches lit no one could see much anyway."

We discussed matters at greater length and I asked him, "Will you still go to Delphi? And is Pylades to go with you?

"Yes he is. We'll make our offerings at Apollo's shrine and from there we'll go to the town of Phocis which is within a day's journey by horse or on foot if we so choose."

"Would Sparta not be better?" I asked. "Surely after what happened to our father Menelaus would be more than willing to help you."

"If he was there, yes, but I hear from traders that he's away from the city and they don't seem to know when he'll be back. Anyway, Pylades says Phocis was his home town before he was adopted and brought to Mycenae."

"His home town – oh, I didn't know that."

"Yes, he remembers much of it and says, or thinks Strophius, who rules the place, was actually his father and his mother was a court woman who died shortly after his birth. He also remembers a visit there of our own father and says he and Strophius would go out hunting together, so it looks like they were good pals. Yes, we'll give Phocis a try first."

"This Strophius I know almost nothing about but it sounds to me a good idea, at least for the time being."

"Right, so all being well we'll keep in touch by messenger, maybe every six months, until I can get back to sort things out here."

"That messenger," I told him, "will need to keep your true whereabouts secret. Meanwhile I'll call for Melia right now and tell her to bring food and drink up here before daylight tomorrow."

"Melia," he grinned, "is she staying the night?"

"No, Orestes, she isn't! And you need your sleep."

***

Orestes left me the following morning. He would meet Pylades outside the palace as he so often did, with both carrying their arms. They would walk down to the Lion Gate as if setting out to continue their training in combat. But instead they would follow the city wall around, perhaps hiring horses, before setting off north-eastwards to pass by Corinth and Megara, enter Boeotia then proceed on the well-established route north-west to Delphi. They planned to stop for rest before reaching Delphi but neither they nor I had any idea where that might be. I watched them from my window as, beneath a cloudless sky, bathed by a newly risen sun, they made their way in the distance toward the woodlands.

With the two of them gone, I felt very much alone. I would confide to no one, not to Chrysothemis, not even to Melia.

Chapter 5
The Fate of Electra

I avoided the great hall, my mother and her darling Aegisthus for the next three days. I met with my friends, one of whom I shared a room with at night in case mother tried to find me. For the same reason I would sometimes meet Chrysothemis in one of the small gardens close to the palace where we would take our food and drink together. It was inevitable that mother would catch up with me sooner or later and on the evening of the fourth day she did so in a corner the dining hall where I had foolishly risked going.

"So here you are hiding away!" she exclaimed, lifting the folds of her open-fronted, regal dress in order to lower herself to a nearby seat. "And your brother – he's not been seen inside or outside the city wall or anywhere else for some time. Rumour has it he's left Mycenae with that friend of his. Am I right; do you know where they've run off to?"

A few people sitting closer to us ceased talking and paused, listening to her raised voice.

I pushed aside my dish. "Left Mycenae!" I exclaimed. "Well, what a surprise. I wonder where he is; not murdered yet like your husband and probably that poor girl Cassandra, I'm pretty sure of that."

This time it was not the wine speaking. The very sight of her and the manner by which she expressed herself aroused my anger. There were drawn breaths, gasps of dismay at my words from those gathered nearby. Mother stared at me for frozen moments without expression then stood up, saying, "Come with me at once, if you please; there is something that needs to be explained and answers I require from you."

I was about to tell her it didn't please me at all but I didn't wish just then to cause more of a scene in front of others, so I got up and followed her, clutching my half-filled goblet. I followed her through the great hall to the reception room situated behind her throne. Its frescoed walls were lit by two burning torches, there were two goblets already set down on the table and filled to the brim with wine. She must earlier have been informed or herself seen me enter the dining hall as it appeared my invitation had been planned in advance.

"What d'you want with me?" I asked.

"I can no longer tolerate your causing me embarrassment in front of others," she declared when seated. "They're beginning to think you've lost your senses, you know. As you evidently have some idea of what happened to your father you should understand fully just why it had to be done. After that I want you to confirm with people what I have already told them – that you had fallen under the influence of that Trojan woman and didn't know quite what you were saying."

"Oh, do go on," I said, downing what was left in the goblet I had carried with me.

"I was there at Aulis," she continued, "I was there when they decided to murder your sister Iphigenia on your father's orders – as if my first

121

born at Pisa wasn't enough. Sacrifice they called it, yes, sacrifice, and done on the advice of that old fool Calchas. But why - why when at night in that foul weather it could have been a goat or some other animal and no one would have realised?" She lifted one of the waiting goblets, drank then added, "Agamemnon did *not* have to do it!"

I took up the other goblet and said, "All I've heard about Pisa are rumours but I'm well aware father was a ruthless killer. I've heard all about what he did at Troy from others who were with him, mainly via Orestes, but I'm *not* convinced over Iphigenia. I heard it said also that he tried to tell you something of importance when he first arrived, Chrysothemis heard him but you wouldn't listen. I wonder what it was he tried to say."

"I recall nothing of the sort," she responded.

"No and you wouldn't want to, would you. You'd already taken Aegisthus to your bed and decided to murder your husband in part to protect him as well as yourself."

"You little -!" she snapped, staring hard at me. "I was a woman ruling my kingdom alone with all the responsibilities and dealings that ought to have been the lot of a warrior king, especially here in Mycenae."

When I said, "Then I take it Periphas wasn't good enough so he had to die did he," she simply refused to respond and gazed for a time into her goblet. When I added, "You play the injured party and, yes, I can understand your grief over Iphigenia if you really did believe her dead but what I don't understand is your willingness to see your own son murdered. Hardly motherly love is it."

She glared at me like a gorgon, as if she wished to turn me to stone, banged down her goblet, spattering the table with wine, rose from her chair and hissed, "Just what d'you mean by *that*?"

"I'll tell you what I mean," I responded, rising to face her, "What I mean is that you're afraid of what Orestes will do to avenge father when he's fully capable so you're content to have Aegisthus and his thugs solve the problem – yes?"

"W-where did you -?"

"Where did I hear it, mother? The gods spoke to me of your plotting in my sleep. Every detail of your conniving with your wonderful Aegisthus they imparted to me and so I warned Orestes. He's left Mycenae with his friend and they've gone to stay elsewhere for as long as necessary."

"Gone *where*?" she demanded, leaning closer to gaze hard and unblinking at me.

"He refused to say where he was going, or maybe he'd not decided, so I have *no* idea – no, none at all! But he will be sending someone here from time to time to make sure I'm all right."

"You really are a conniving little bitch," she muttered, tugging at her dress. "Never mind the gods – you've somehow been spying on me – on us. I'll need to watch you, won't I – yes every hour of every day I'll have to keep an eye on you." The torch flames swayed as she turned and swished from the room. I was once more alone and far from contented.

***

'She informed me Orestes had left the city with that friend of his but couldn't or wouldn't say where he was going. She claims he refused to tell her or that he didn't know.'

They sat alone in Clytemnestra's main room and gazed out across a moonlit landscape.

'Perhaps they're headed for Sparta,' said Aegisthus, raising the ornately gilded wine cup to his lips.

'Perhaps so; he might well find sympathy and backing there even though Menelaus may still be involved in some petty campaign or other - or so I hear. And when he does return he will not be pleased to learn from Orestes about his own brother's death here in Mycenae. Orestes intends to have someone come to Mycenae to contact Electra but we don't know who or when. Meanwhile, what I'd like to know is how Electra found out what she did. It's as if someone overheard every word of our conversation but – but who and - and how?'

'Yes, who and how?' breathed Aegisthus. 'And if Orestes ends up in Sparta he may have them raise men against us. I'll send two of my own men as traders and if Orestes is there and Menelaus is still absent they can solve the problem before it occurs, don't you think? Then the account of Agamemnon's death can be maintained as we consider fit.'

Clytemnestra continued to stare beyond the window into darkness then answered, 'Yes, if that's what has to be done, then - then so be it.'

'You sound hesitant,' said Aegisthus, 'but you know Orestes' feelings toward you and me well enough. He'd see both of us dead after what happened here.'

'You first, I imagine,' she muttered.

'And what about Electra? She'll have suitors clamouring at our gates just as her sister does.'

'Chrysothemis desires only to marry and get away from here, and nothing more, so the sooner the better. Electra has always had her admirers but wants before anything else to see us out of the way and Orestes on the throne. She's said far too much already and refuses to help in putting matters right. I now have to take care she causes no further mischief. I'll turn away any suitors or I'll tell them she's accounted for and I'll ensure she's confined within the palace where I can keep an eye on her. I'll have her supervised day by day by my own attendants."

"Are you saying you'll make her a prisoner?"

"I see no other way, and *you* have to stay well clear of her! Do you understand?'

'As you wish,' he shrugged, downing more wine, 'but at her age she'll be wanting a man. Maybe one of the palace guards will have to pay her a -.' Clytemnestra's expression of disapproval stalled his words but then he asked, 'And what happens when someone is sent by her brother to speak with her?'

'I'd suggest you use your imagination but don't bother - I have already planned for that event. So if and when that someone does arrive here you'd better keep out of the way. Meanwhile, Aegisthus, dear, I'd say you've had quite enough to drink. Let's get to bed shall we.'

***

The breezes were cooler and rain had fallen earlier that morning when three strangers on horseback entered the palace courtyard and there drew to a halt. Watched by four guards standing by the entrance they dismounted, two in plain tunics, though well-armed, taking charge of the horses, while the third in more formal attire and bearing a staff of office, approached the guards. He trod the short flight of steps then halted before them to announce, 'I am Pedaeus; I am sent by Orestes, true son of Agamemnon and brother of Lady Electra. He wishes me to deliver his message to Lady Electra and requests that she gives me a message for him in return.'

Two of the guards conducted Pedaeus into the anteroom where one remained at his side and the other stepped through into the megaron. The envoy waited, expecting soon there would be a summons to enter the great hall where he would accomplish his task. He had grown impatient when a courtier, accompanied by the guard, stepped from the megaron to inform him that, 'Food and wine are made ready for you here and will be offered also to your companions waiting outside. Lady Electra will be with you soon. After you have spoken with her you and your men may, should you so wish, remain here in the palace until tomorrow morning.'

This formality he might have expected as was a possible if modest presentation of gifts, though he had brought only small items for Electra herself. Following the courtier across the megaron and by the great hearth where a warming fire danced brightly, he observed the throne and lesser seat to be unoccupied. Passing to the rear of these he was conducted to the private reception room where a cold meal and a goblet of wine awaited. There he sat, taking what was offered but puzzled that no one of real authority had so far greeted him.

His food was finished and his goblet empty when the door opened and she entered. Pedaeus arose to face a slim blue-eyed girl in her late teens. Corn-blond hair fell about the shoulders of her colourfully embroidered dress and she regarded the envoy without expression as he offered a slight bow and said, 'Ah, Lady Electra, you are just as your brother Orestes described. I am Pedaeus, I am instructed to offer you his greetings, to offer you gifts and to ask after your own situation.'

From a pouch in his robe he withdrew and unwrapped a pair of golden, jewel-studded clasps intended to embellish and hold back her hair. She stared down and reached to take the gift from him as if doubting whether she ought to do so, then smiled, 'You may tell Orestes that I thank him for these, that I am in good health and that I sorely miss his company. I pray to the gods each day for his wellbeing and for his return to Mycenae once danger has passed.'

'Danger?' queried the envoy.

'There is much danger, yes; that is why he left Mycenae. There are others here in the city ready to conspire against him though his mother, Lady Clytemnestra, has denounced them and much regrets all that has happened. But my dear brother –

is he well, and where now is he? That I have to know for my own peace of mind.'

'He is well indeed but wishes no one to know where he presently resides.'

The girl's expression hardened. 'Tell me where my brother is,' she demanded, 'tell me now. Why should I, his sister, not know this?'

'Madam,' he answered, 'I could not tell you even if I wanted to. Your brother and I met by prior arrangement at a village of small consequence in Boeotia so I am no wiser than are you as to his actual whereabouts.' The girl waited as if not knowing what next to say, so the envoy continued, 'Your brother asks also about your sister, Chrysothemis. Is she well and is she still here in Mycenae?'

'Chrysothemis?' she responded with some hesitation before answering, 'Oh, yes, she married a noble of the Corinthian ruling house and now lives there. We hear she is indeed well.'

'You yourself must have many suitors,' smiled Pedaeus. 'Has Lady Clytemnestra on your behalf or you yourself felt inclined to consider any of these men?'

'None at all, no. None of them are considered appropriate.' She eyed him nervously then said, 'I must go now; I have much to discuss with Lady Clytemnestra.'

Left alone, Pedaeus continued to stare at the door for some time after it had closed. He then made his way from the chamber and through the almost deserted Megaron, speaking to no one and noting the throne still unoccupied before re-joining his companions. At first light the following day they would leave Mycenae.

***

The sun was past is zenith when, in the only tavern of a rustic village the three sat grouped about a table with rough terracotta cups containing an equally rough wine.

'Lady Electra assured me she was in good health and she certainly appeared so,' said the envoy. 'She was amiable enough until questioning me over your whereabouts. When I was unable to give her an answer she became rather agitated.'

'Did she now. That's strange, yes, strange indeed because I had told her before I left Mycenae where I intended to go.'

'Very strange,' shrugged Pylades. 'Perhaps she'd forgotten.'

'Hmm, perhaps she had, as you say, forgotten,' muttered Orestes.

'And,' Pedaeus continued, 'she spoke of danger should you return and advised, sir, against your doing so.'

'Oh, really - that I do know about and I'm well aware as to who is behind it.'

'She told me also that your mother regretted what had happened there before you left.'

'That I find difficult to believe,' breathed Orestes. 'The gods must have turned her mind. And what news have you of Chrysothemis?'

'Lady Electra seemed at first vague about your other sister though did inform me she had married a noble of Corinth and now lived there.' Pedaeus sipped his wine, peered dubiously into the cup,

129

pushed it dismissively aside then added, 'I confess I felt something was not quite as it ought to be but I cannot say for certain why.'

'Did you now; but you were convinced it really was my sister were you not? Even so I'm beginning to wonder if all was as well as she claimed.'

'I'd certainly be wondering,' added Pylades, pushing aside his own cup. 'But then she may have been a bit nervous for some reason or other.'

'Well, sir -,' replied the envoy, raising his hands before Orestes, 'well she was most certainly as you described in age and appearance even if somewhat reserved in her manner. I therefore cannot claim she was anything other than your sister, Lady Electra.'

'Then I can only hope for now,' said Orestes, 'that she is safe and well. Meanwhile we must continue your visits and hope the situation becomes clearer.'

***

I of course knew nothing of the messenger for by then I was hardly more than a prisoner, restricted by order of my mother much of the day to the area of my own rooms and no longer able to meet with my friends. At the bottom of the stairs leading to the ground floor she had placed a guard. Was it one of Aegisthus' men I wondered? I was left largely to my own devices though with at first an occasional visit from Melia, who at least did her best to console me. When her visits ended I suspected mother's denial to me of her company was in case I persuaded her by whatever means to act as a go-between and seek out my brother via the envoy when he next arrived. Now I felt truly alone. It was worse at night as you might expect. I thought of Orestes and his light-hearted and often boastful ways. I thought of Pylades, his boyhood friend. Pylades, who I liked very much and also missed.

Food and drink were brought up to me morning and evening by two of mother's appointed attendants. Both were older women who were at first bereft of amiable conversation even when they kept me company. Sometimes I was allowed down into the dining hall to eat when all others had gone but not into the megaron. Escorted access to one of the small gardens was permitted on occasion and there I was allowed a breath of freedom, though at such times other people were denied access by a guard posted at the entrance. When confined upstairs I would often sit at my loom, at other times by my window to gaze across town and countryside. I watched people come and go and for a while hoped one of them would bring me news from Phocis. Then there were questions. How did mother explain my situation to others in the palace and to my companions for surely I would be glimpsed from time to time when going outside? Had she earlier threatened Melia not to discuss me with anyone, even with my friends? And *where* was the promised messenger from Orestes?

Now and again mother would visit me hoping, so I imagined, to regain my trust but I was unable to offer her what I did not possess and pretending to do so was not within me. One day as I sat at my loom, she walked in and asked, "Why do you punish yourself by continuing to act as you do? You must come to terms with what happened because it had to be."

"Had to be?" I responded, rising to face her. "No, it was brutal murder by you and that – that contemptible man you share your bed with! It was so with Periphas and I know one of you, Aegisthus or most likely one of his thugs, murdered Cassandra! If that's not true then deny it – go on, deny it to my face! The gods above know what you and that man really are and I pray each day they will bring retribution down upon you both."

Her expression might have been carved from hard stone. She turned without another word and left the room. I knew even before the door slammed I should not have antagonised her further; perhaps she might eventually have had Leucon visit me to play his lyre or permitted the return of Melia. Then I began to wonder if Melia was safe. Now I could expect little other than increased loneliness for mother did not visit me again. I feared after that final encounter she might have me locked inside because my door, like others, could be bolted from the outside as well as from within, but she did not. Leaving my door ajar gave me at least the illusion of a freedom I otherwise did not have. There were, of course, two other chambers close to mine, left empty though not bare, one having belonged to Orestes, the other to Chrysothemis where some of her clothes and personal possessions remained in an old wooden chest. Nobody had used those rooms since the two had departed. I sometimes entered one of them where I would stand alone in all enveloping silence and call upon memories, but even though bed and bath remained ready for use in each, there were few other comforts to be had and only nameless ghosts stirred within the shadows.

In time those women appointed by my mother to oversee my life had begun to treat me with some consideration and would often remain longer with me in conversation indoors, as well as out. We discussed the gods, their wiles and their ways; something I had taken only a passing interest in before but now had time to think about. Both of them, I learned, served at the temple of Zeus, keeping the place clean, so I imagined. They offered me but passing news of the world beyond, however, and claimed to know nothing of any messenger, which I believed was so. Wine they did bring me, and in liberal quantity, so that it often dulled my senses. I imagined that was what they or more likely my mother wanted. One thing I eventually did learn, and it saddened me greatly, was that dear old Leucon had died peacefully in his bed.

Time became an increasing burden, especially through the winter days, and I could only wait until the cooler days passed and the skies grew brighter. I would often look across the city where smoke drifted up from tavern and workshop. There was sound and life down there; all of it denied to me. Working at my loom helped the days pass by but these seemed now endless. I had nothing to offer by way of sacrifice but during my many restless nights I gave prayer to almighty Zeus and to Hera, his consort. I begged for Orestes to somehow contact me but it did not happen. I wished I could sneak down to the megaron to ask if any messenger had arrived but there was always a guard at the bottom of the stairs.

Months passed by, then seasons and hardly anything in my existence changed. The loom continued to occupy much of my day when I was left alone and dyed yarn was sent up to me when I asked for it. And what was I weaving? Lengths of material for someone else to make into garments or whatever pleased them. By then I really didn't care. The months rolled into seasons and the seasons into years. Seven long, numbing years. Seven years that were an eternity and I was then aged twenty-five. Each morning when I arose to stare out over this grim city the sunlit fields and woodlands, the hills beyond, all mocked me as an unattainable dream. The peasants and even most of the palace slaves possessed more freedom than I did.

Sometimes when soaking in my bath I would stare up at those sea creatures painted on my walls and imagine myself as one of them, gliding blissfully through the waters. Each morning I would peer into my bronze mirror. Now and again I would talk to my own reflection and ask myself who I was and why I existed. I would sit and brush my hair, occasionally trimmed by one of those women. I brushed it to convince myself and them that I still believed in life.

I was by then drinking more wine than ever. My existence, my very being had become meaningless and so lost and despairing was I during that seventh year that it seemed I might as well bring this whole wretched affair to an end. Often I would lean out of my window to peer down at the stone courtyard below. It might take some courage but in those brief, exhilarating moments of ecstasy I would fly free like a bird. But no, I couldn't do that. I didn't want to be discovered, my body shattered and bleeding, by people who would stand about to point and indulge in mindless gossip. There was my bath. I could tap hot water and almost fill it. Yes, I would drink enough wine to render myself senseless. I would sink beneath the water into warm, caressing depths of endless sleep. I imagined someone entering the room to see my image on the frescoed wall above the bath, leaping with the dolphins. Such thoughts were beginning to possess me but, then, something quite, something utterly incredible happened.

Late one afternoon as I sat bowed in tearful misery I heard footsteps outside and I looked up expecting to see those two women enter the room. But when the door opened, there stood Chrysothemis. Yes, Chrysothemis! I gasped, thinking for a moment this must be a dream or a cruel illusion, a result of too much wine.

"Oh, what a long time it's been, sister dear," she smiled, stepping over to me. I arose unsteadily, a hand gripping the edge of my table. I gaped at her open-mouthed and was quite lost for words.

We each stared at the other until at last I was able to speak. "W-what are you doing here? How did you -? What is happening?"

"You look at me as if I'm Medusa," she grinned, placing her arms about my waist. "Aren't you glad to see me? I returned today from Corinth in the company of traders with two of my friends.

135

And you – you look so pale and I find you in tears. By now you should be married and gone away from Mycenae. It's been many years since I left."

"Over seven," I breathed clasping her in turn. "But how did you get up here unchallenged?"

"How?" she smiled, "Well, the way I always used to of course. I entered the megaron; there were a few people there but no sign of mother or that wretched man who I know is still around. Everything felt so strange, none of them took much notice of me, Leucon was nowhere to be seen and when I asked about you they made out they'd seen hardly anything of you in ages and weren't sure exactly where you were. One of them told me our mother was away in Argos until tomorrow and Aegisthus was out hunting so I came up here on the off-chance hoping you might be around. There's an armed man sitting near the bottom of the stairs. He appeared perfectly drunk and half tried to stop me as I slipped past him but that was all. I've no idea what he was doing there. Now you tell me – *what is* going on?"

My mind buzzing I stepped over to close the door, turned and said, "Oh, if only you knew what has -. Look, we need to keep our voices down." I offered her what little wine I had left but thought it was not a good idea just then to call for more, something I was otherwise permitted to do as often as I wished. So with me pulling myself together and listening for voices or footsteps in the corridor outside, we sat close to one another and I explained as best and as briefly as I could what had given rise to my situation and what I had endured since her leaving Mycenae. "Had either of them been down there, had mother or Aegisthus seen you," I assured her, "they would most certainly have prevented you from coming up to find me, I'm certain of that. And if my attendants find you here they will call for that guard whether he's drunk or not."

"But, Electra, dear, all these years of torment! This is - this is utterly dreadful. Why did you not leave Mycenae when you had the chance?"

"I was, I still am and I always will be driven by a hatred of them both. I was determined to see them punished but that has instead brought about my present situation and I have achieved nothing."

"You should have left well alone as did I."

"No, that I could never do. So now – tell me about yourself."

"I was married in Corinth to one of the king's numerous sons but nothing came of it; I bore him no children, which soured our relationship, so we came to live almost separate lives and he took other women. He was killed in some petty conflict with pirates and after that I no longer had reason to stay in Corinth though it's there I still remain for the time being. I had no more suitors because it was said by those who claim to know about these things that I would never bear a son. Orestes visited the city over a year ago and sought me out there. He is a grown man, fit and strong, a true warrior and you'd be proud of him. I'd say he's another Achilles but more thoughtful and considerate. He told me how he and his friend, Pylades, now serve the King of Phocis directly as his personal guard and are most highly thought of. We of course discussed you. He

137

told me messengers had contacted you and you in turn had informed them you were keeping well but were insistent upon his not returning to Mycenae. He's questioned traders who visit Mycenae but none of them have been able to help him."

"I have seen *no* messengers," I assured her. "None in all since Orestes left."

"Then both you and our brother have been much deceived over these past years."

"We must get word to Orestes," I said. "Can you somehow do that before anyone realises you've been able to contact me? Mother won't let me leave these rooms without her women and it's why that man is waiting on the stairs below. I think he, and sometimes one of the others, are those brought into the palace by Aegisthus so he won't know who you are."

"Those two friends I mentioned," she replied, "one of them, Eriphia, knows Phocis well but Phocis is, I think, a three day's journey from Mycenae and probably too unsafe a route for women unless we join a party." I remained silent as Chrysothemis considered what best to do. At last she said, "Much as I hate to become involved this cannot go on – not with my own sister being denied her freedom."

"When did you say our dear mother returns?" I asked.

"Later tomorrow someone said, so we'll need to keep out of her way. My friends and I will if possible find somewhere to refresh ourselves and remain within the palace or one of the temples for the night. We can pay for whatever we have but taverns are out of the question. At daybreak we'll leave the city and find a party going to Delphi – there are always people going to Delphi, and from there we'll go on to Phocis. We have gold pieces aplenty, as much as we need, so you must come with us."

I considered her words then said, "No, those two women who come up here would raise the alarm. And that guard down below might recognise me, drunk or no, and that would endanger both of us. We must arouse no suspicions. I would prefer Orestes to find his way here unnoticed and at night if at all possible."

"Please, Electra, the man down there was half asleep. You can wait until those women have been and gone then you don't have to stay any longer."

"I must stay for all our sakes. When they discover I'm gone Aegisthus will find out where we left from and which party we were with. He'll send out armed horsemen who would easily catch up with us. What difference can a few more days make after all these years."

"Very well," responded Chrysothemis, "then once we get to Phocis I'll explain to Orestes what they've done to you. He will wish to return here but in case he has duties or problems that cannot be abandoned we should give him enough time – say, seven days."

"Very well," I agreed, "seven days – a day for each full year I've been kept here. So for now, if that guard is still half senseless and as you're all girls you may be able to get your two friends by him and stay with me. He'll maybe think you've had permission from our mother anyway as you're heading up here - but be careful. You can hide when needs be in your and Orestes' old rooms. But - but in the morning there will be another man on the stairs. You'll be going down and he'll probably be sober so I wonder what will happen then. No, this is all too risky; maybe you *would* be better off somewhere else."

"We have to try," she smiled. "If needs be we'll say we lost our way in the palace and promise not to report him for failing to attend to his duty. Eriphia's rather good at charming men – you'll see what I mean. By the time he decides what to do we'll be gone and of course he won't want to follow us in case you slip out."

"Well alright, but you'd better get past him now before he's properly awake or those women come up here with my food. Grab yourselves something from the kitchens; that shouldn't be too difficult if they take you as courtiers. There'll also be a jug of wine on one of the tables."

Chrysothemis kissed and left me but though the day was late a blaze of hope flooded through to illuminate what had been so much a prison for all those years and I lived again. Truly, I was elated beyond measure! I don't recall Chrysothemis ever before showed such initiative but though risky it simply *had* to work. I stood listening by the part-opened door. I heard noises downstairs but it seemed an eternity before I heard footsteps and for heart-beating moments I could not be sure who it was approaching; my female keepers perhaps, though it ought to have been too early for them.

140

Then my sister and her two companions appeared from the gloom of the stairs, bringing between them an amphora and dishes of food which they carried in to all but obscure the top of my small table. She next introduced me to her friends. They were some years younger than ourselves, bright and cheerful, but it was fair-haired, heavily perfumed Eriphia who struck me as quite alluring in both appearance and manner as she smiled then stooped to regard herself in my mirror. Dark-haired Phoebe, the other girl, was slim and pretty but would prove somewhat reserved. Both, of course, were understandably puzzled over what was happening.

"We held back in the passage below until your guard slipped away to relive himself," Chrysothemis informed me. "Better than letting him see us."

"So now we can set to and enjoy ourselves," grinned Eriphia. "Lovely to meet you."

"Lovely to meet you, too," smiled Phoebe.

"No, we have to wait," I insisted. "Hide in one of the empty rooms until those women have been and gone. Take in there everything you brought with you and I'll call for you as soon as they've left."

The sun was well down when the two women did arrive. I feigned indifference, I told them I was tired but all the time I was afraid there might be something remaining in the room to give away my visitors presence.

"That's a strong perfume you're wearing, your ladyship," remarked one of them sarcastically as they placed down my food and drink. "Not expecting a man are you?"

"If only," I replied. "No, it's just something to please the gods – Apollo, maybe, since I've used up all my incense sticks." That was true, I had none left.

To my relief, on sensing my reluctance to converse, the unwelcome pair said nothing more about the perfume and stayed no longer than they felt necessary. I nevertheless waited a while before leaving my room to summon back Chrysothemis, Eriphia and Phoebe. Soon enough, with the rest of my lamps burning and my window blind in place, I and my three wonderful visitors were able to enjoy ourselves with wine and subdued, conversation.

"In seven days," I said, "yes, in seven days from tomorrow you promise me Orestes will return, seven days from when you leave the city." I wanted to hear myself say those words then I added, "But tell him not to risk entering the palace; say I will wait for him at night in the grave circle where our father is buried."

"But whether he's sober or not," said Chrysothemis, "you are one person the guard downstairs and other people will recognise. He might not disappear for a while as he did for us."

"Maybe, but I'll find a way out of here – somehow. If he doesn't wander off to relive himself I think I know what to do."

The next morning they also would have to leave unchallenged and that, for the time being, was my only concern. During the night I would pray to almighty Zeus and to Hera and ask for further blessings.

***

'We'd better not risk all three of us trying to get past him again,' Chrysothemis had earlier advised. 'Whoever is down there may be more alert this morning as Electra says.'

The sky beyond Electra's window was lightening as Eriphia pulled on and adjusted a dress chosen from among others left in Chrysothemis' old room, a colourfully flounced, short-sleeved court dress of a noblewoman, a dress that left her firm breasts exposed. Red-lipped, perfumed Eriphia, her hair pinned up before my mirror in a semblance of Cretan style, stepped out into the corridor. From there she felt her way cautiously and quietly down the dark stairs then, turning the corner, observed the guard, illuminated only by the flame of a single torch. He was seated, resting against the wall, breathing heavily, his eyes closed, his bronze-tipped spear propped diagonally with its blade against the opposite wall. Eriphia held her breath, tilted the spear away so as ease slowly past him then let it back again. She coughed lightly then as he began to awaken she looked down at him and said, 'Excuse me, sir.'

The guard mumbled, stirred, opened his eyes, looked up at her, blinked and wondered if what he saw before him was a divine visitation.

'Excuse me,' she repeated as the man continued to gape, 'I am instructed to await Lord Aegisthus in the great hall but I'm lost. I wonder if you could show me the way.'

The guard continued to regard her with lust in his eyes but smiling broadly, grasped his spear and heaved himself up saying, 'Show you the way - right, yeah.' As Eriphia followed in his echoing footsteps from one dim corridor to another he grinned back at her with irregular, discoloured teeth, adding, 'You come back later, goddess, an' I'll show you somethin' else.'

They passed through the ante-room and reached the entrance to the deserted megaron where Eriphia said with a bright-eyed smile, 'Ah, so this is it – but where is Lord Aegisthus? I see no one on the throne.'

'Wait an' 'e'll be down 'ere soon enough – not long now I'd say.'

Eriphia thanked him once more and the guard, glancing twice back at her, would return to his allotted position at the base of the stairs with Eriphia's image a shimmering flame in his mind. As he passed by he failed to see, concealed within the deeper shadows of a colonnade, two figures clutching leather satchels. Once he was gone they hurried along to the ante-room where Eriphia waited and Chrysothemis, pulling open her satchel, said to her, 'Quick, get changed; we'll all wear plain clothes so we don't attract anyone's attention. People will already be entering the city to set up their wares in the marketplace.'

A band of light defined the eastern horizon as they left the palace unchallenged to walk down the great stone ramp and out through the Lion Gate where merchants and traders, their carts full of goods were already rumbling by. Armed guards at the gate eyed them with curiosity but made no attempt to hinder their progress.

'There will be people gathering by the stables,' said Chrysothemis. 'If the gods are with us we should soon be able to join a group leaving for Delphi.'

The bright eye of Helios peered upon them from over the hills as they negotiated a place with their chosen party of some twelve men, each armed with sword, some also with spear. Most would occupy carts drawn by asses but three would ride on horseback, these being fully armed warriors, each with plumed helmets of interlocking boars' tusks, boiled leather corselet and at his left a small round shield with bronze boss. They were a reassuring sight to Chrysothemis, Eriphia and Phoebe.

'You women,' remarked one of the burly and bearded horsemen as the party prepared to move off, 'you all 'eaded just for Delphi, then? It's not women usually goes there except to entertain in some of the taverns, if y'get my meanin'.'

'Not to Delphi, no,' responded Chrysothemis. 'From there we go on to Phocis.'

'Right, then that's not so far away from where we're goin' is it; under 'alf a day from Delphi on 'orse an' the route'll be clear enough. We'll 'ave you' all of the way safe an' sound to Delphi an' there you'll be safe to stay the night.' He raised his spear and called, 'Right – let's get movin' – we've two days 'ead of us!'

**

From my window I watched them depart in morning sunlight. All three were in one of the carts, I recognised their gowns but I couldn't tell from so far away who was who. I continued to gaze out, seeing them move north-east until their party had vanished amid woodlands. I had not heard the door open behind me but turned to face both of my appointed keepers with their copper trays.

"Admiring the world outside, are we, dear?" asked one of them as they placed my morning food and drink onto the table.

"Lovely day for a walk in the woods, isn't it," I remarked, trying not to sound too sarcastic.

"Lady Clytemnestra says you may spend more time in the garden this afternoon; that'll be nice, won't it."

"Her kindness overwhelms me," I responded.

"Down in the depths of misery she was 'til yesterday," commented the other. "Wonder what's 'appened since then."

"D'you fancy talking for a while?" asked her companion.

I normally would have agreed but this time I answered, "No, maybe later." I had over the years accepted their company and at times secretly welcomed it, thinking of them as rather domineering aunts, for although they were obeying orders from mother they seemed never to have borne me ill will. Oddly, I had learned but never used their names, perhaps because it might have implied a degree of friendship and trust I did not want to nurture. When they were gone I gazed once more from my window into a world that at long, long last offered hope.

***

Having remained overnight in a pilgrims' hostel at Delphi, Chrysothemis, Eriphia and Phoebe journeyed by wagon to Phocis in the company of a returning delegation sent to Delphi the previous day. Chrysothemis inquired about her brother from members of their party and they confirmed his status in their town. On passing through the city gate it was Eriphia, with her knowledge of Phocis, who walked before them to the palace; a more modest, less imposing building than that in which Electra languished. To Chrysothemis' eye this town, though strongly fortified, was a more welcoming sight than had been Mycenae. On reaching the palace it was sweet-smiling Eriphia who ascended the steps where she requested one of the guards to inform Orestes that his sister, Chrysothemis, had arrived from Mycenae and awaited him.

'I hope he isn't out hunting,' said Chrysothemis as the guard disappeared into the building.

'I don't recall ever seeing your brother,' remarked Phoebe. 'Is he handsome?'

'Most girls seemed to think so as I remember but you'll have to make your own mind up. Try smiling at him like the way Eriphia smiles at men – but don't make it too obvious; he'll be used to that kind of thing, I'm sure.'

They lapsed into silence and watched the palace entrance where a grinning Eriphia stood in conversation with the remaining guard who appeared to indulge her with more attention than his duty required. They ceased talking and stepped aside as two figures emerged, one being the first guard, the other a well-built young man in his early twenties who paused to greet and exchange words with Eriphia. His eyes were sharp, has face clean-shaven and framed by fair, shoulder-length hair held in place by a blue linen band, his expression one of confidence and determination. His white tunic was colourfully embroidered at collar and hem and from his finely tooled belt swung an intricately wrought scabbard in which rested a sword with ornate inlay at its hilt and precious stone at its pommel. Eriphia followed close as, an arm raised in greeting, a broad smile on his face, Orestes strode from the palace steps to halt before Chrysothemis who he hugged and kissed before offering a polite nod to shy but admiring Phoebe. Eriphia stood to assess him also with a coquettish smile as he turned back to Chrysothemis, saying, 'The last I heard you were still in Corinth but I'm surprised and mightily pleased to see you – and your friends. I'm told you've travelled all the way from Mycenae. You must come and take wine with me but first I have to ask about Electra as you must have spoken with her. Tell me, is all well with our sister after all this time? My envoy is not due to visit Mycenae for another month or more but the messages he brings back have had me thinking there is more I ought to know.'

'All is not well with Electra,' Chrysothemis responded, 'and never has been since you left Mycenae. May we talk somewhere other than here?'

Orestes' smile gave way to an expression of concern as he replied, 'Yes, of course - follow me.' He conducted them into the palace, through a colonnaded passage then into a small, shaded courtyard where colourful plants grew in decorated ceramic pots and wooden seats awaited. There they sat, bathed in afternoon sunlight, and Orestes said, 'Tell me then, why is all not well with Electra and what really is happening in Mycenae? I hear news from traders but nothing of any real interest.'

'The man you've been sending these past years to speak with her,' answered Chrysothemis, 'has never, *ever* seen Electra and she knows absolutely nothing of him.'

'Knows nothing of him!' Orestes exclaimed. 'How is this and what's happened to her?'

'The one seen by your messenger is a woman similar in appearance to our sister and instructed by our mother to give him false information.'

'Is *that* so – then tell me everything.'

'When you were gone, Electra accused our mother openly, yes, before the whole court she accused her of murder and adultery. Because of this she's been kept a virtual prisoner for over seven years and allowed to see no one except for mother's own attendants who bring her food and take her outside for sunlight and fresh air. I - we discovered this only a few days ago. We have to help her, Orestes, really we do. The most fruitful years of her life have been denied her by our own spiteful mother and it seems not so long ago our poor sister thought to take her own life.'

Orestes leaned back, stared at Chrysothemis a while then said, 'If all this is true, and I doubt not a single word of it, then I've been greatly deceived. I've been deceived and now I'm much angered. The guilt here is also mine for letting the years go by

149

without pressing harder for more information. Yes, I have allowed affairs here at Phocis to occupy too much of my attention. I will return to Mycenae and deal with matters there once and for all.'

'I told her you would be there on the seventh day after our leaving Mycenae,' said Chrysothemis. 'Electra says she will meet with you after sunset by our father's grave in the big circle. They keep a guard on the stairs below her room but whether he sleeps or not Electra says she will find a way to get past him.'

'Well if she can't do that I'll find my way into there and see to it the man sleeps for good.'

'We'll go back with you,' said Eriphia. 'Perhaps we can help in some way.'

Orestes eyed each of them in turn and muttered, 'Hm, if you must.'

Chapter 6
The Return of Orestes

I counted the days from Chrysothemis' visit with a mixture of hope and trepidation. I took a length of wool and for each passing sunset I tied a knot in it. I was afraid those women might read the change in my mood and suspect something so I was usually at my loom when they came to visit me. Otherwise I would sit by the window, gazing over the fields and woodlands in the direction from which Orestes would most likely approach, even though I knew it would probably be in disguise or at night.

When at last the seventh day arrived I was hardly able to conceal my agitation. In the morning the two women arrived with my food and drink, their intention being to conduct me when I'd finished eating to the small garden which would as always be cleared of other people. There I might converse with them but if not I would otherwise stroll about in circles or sit listening to the birds while the women chatted between themselves. On that morning I avoided conversation and was back in my rooms by midday.

Later that day, with the sun low on the horizon, they reappeared as expected. I was sitting with my elbows placed on the table, my head lowered and resting on my hands. I raised up and watched as they placed the trays on my table but I ignored the food and drink. I didn't thank them but then I very rarely had.

"Are you feeling unwell?" asked one of them.

I waited several heartbeats then looked up at her saying, "Please, I find I cannot sleep of late. I need something other than just wine to help me do so."

"You've been all right until now have you not," she responded.

"She was very quiet this morning," said her companion. "Perhaps it's the food."

"She gets the same food as ourselves and most of those in our court – some of the best food in the palace."

"When you've finished discussing me," I said, "perhaps you could offer me some help to obtain proper rest; it's a part of your job isn't it – looking after me, I mean. What does my dear mother take when guilt threatens to keep her awake, as it must all too often do?"

They considered my question and one answered, "There is a potion supplied by one of our priests; we add this to Lady Clytemnestra's wine on those occasions when she requests it. I will fetch some now if that's what you need."

She was gone and I was left with her companion. I feigned tiredness and so we spoke little. After a while the other woman returned with a small ceramic flask. This she placed by the jug of wine on my table, saying, "Add no more than a half of this to the whole of your wine jar and keep the remainder for another time. It is quite strong."

"We don't want her sleeping through most of tomorrow, do we," commented the other.

They stood looking down at me a while longer then left. By now the sky was darkening and thoughts of what I had to do were firm in my mind, though I was very much afraid. From the small lamp that was always burning in my main room I lit three others. Holding one of these I opened my main door, peered out then stepped along the outside passage to enter Chrysothemis' old rooms. Once inside I recovered one of the three goblets hidden out of sight there after use by my visitors, then I returned to where I belonged. Sitting before the table I picked up the wine jar and filled my own goblet half way. The potion, or whatever it was that woman had brought me, I poured into the jug of remaining wine. Yes, every drop of it. I stood up and I was shaking. I left my seat, returned to the passage and walked those few steps along to face stairs that descended into utter darkness. I felt cold, mainly with fear I suppose, though I had on only a gown of fine cotton and a pair of soft shoes. Raising my lamp with one hand, the other pressed to cold stone, I trod carefully down, turning to peer around the corner until, by the light of the firebrand in the lower corridor, I was able to see the guard appointed for the night. Should I wait? He might need to go and relieve himself and I could be away. Then he might not and the night would be passing by. No, I had to risk doing what I had planned. He was not fully armed as they sometimes were, that is, he had no spear with which to bar anyone's way. He rested on the lower step with his back against the wall but he was fully awake. He eased himself to his feet, stared up at me and asked, "An' where d'you think your goin'? No one leaves by 'ere without say-so, lady; that's my orders. Get back up there now.'

"I wasn't trying to get past you," I said, "I wondered if I might offer you a cup of wine. I have more than I need and – and I thought, being alone as you are and stuck here until morning, you might care to accept my offer."

He ran a hand down over his beard, seeming for the moment lost for words, then asked, "Where is it then – this wine?"

"Oh, it's in my room of course. If you want to follow me perhaps you could keep me company for a while; I feel so very lonely at times."

"Taken you a good while to ask me that 'asn't it?" he grinned. "I've been on duty on an' off night times down 'ere for two years an' more."

"Well -?" I queried, wondering what he must have thought of me standing there in the lurid glow of the torch in my flimsy, clinging dress. Was this one of the five men called in by Aegisthus? Listening to his speech I thought somehow it was not.

"I'll not follow you up there," he answered, resolutely, "No - I'm ordered not to do that by Lady Clytemnestra and Lord Aegisthus - on pain of death as it 'appens. Aye, pain of death they said."

"And who could possibly know what you do at this time of the night," I assured him. "I certainly wouldn't say anything because I would also suffer. Anyway, you wouldn't be the first."

He peered along the lower corridor again, back at me then once more ran a hand over his beard. The light of desire glowed in his eyes as he said in a low voice, "Wouldn't be the first, eh. Then maybe for a short while - aye, maybe just a while."

I turned around to ascend the stairs and heard the heavy clump of his boots as he started to follow me. We entered my chamber and, with the door closed, he stood looking about, seeming almost as apprehensive as I was. "You must first take some wine," I said, pouring a generous measure into the spare goblet, "then we may stay together a while." He accepted the goblet and downed almost a half of its contents at once; a man most ill at ease he obviously was. I drank more of my own wine then asked, "What is your name?"

He gulped back the rest of his wine then replied, "It's Byzas, that's me name."

"Well Byzas," I said as he reached out a trembling hand to stroke my breast, "you appear most uneasy and that will not do. If we're to enjoy each other's company tonight then you must relax and take a little more wine." I gripped the wine jar hard, replenished his goblet and thought, "If this doesn't work the night will be a disaster from which I'll never recover." He drank back his second goblet of wine almost as quickly as he had the first then stood eyeing me up and down with carnal anticipation "Now, Byzas," I said, "you really have to feel at ease. Go through there and rest on my bed and I'll be with you very soon."

"Aye, right, I'll do that," he answered, grinning broadly as I showed him into the next room where the three oil lamps burned. He tugged off his leather boots, fell back onto the bed with a long sigh and,

155

still smiling, closed his eyes. Whatever the effect of the potion I had to move quickly. I pulled on a warmer, cowled gown of plain appearance I'd laid aside ready to cover the dress I was wearing then on went my warm ankle boots. I hesitated and listened. There was only silence but I felt compelled to look into the room where Byzas lay. As I peered tentatively around the door I could hear him snoring. I tip-toed across the room. My heart beating hard as holding up my lamp I stepped through the outer door and closed it gently. Now at last I could escape! But I wavered once again, gazed at the outer bolts, one close to the top, the other well below the centre of the door. I reached and with no small effort I slid both bolts shut. The grating sound they made echoed down the stairs. I waited, I listened, but hearing no other sounds I trod the steps until the firebrand close to their base, and others placed further along, made my way clearer. Now with enough light, I laid aside my lamp, pulled the cowl over my head then hurried on until reaching the entrance to the megaron because this was the route I had to follow. Stepping cautiously by I glanced aside to see both the throne and the seat next to it vacant. The fire in the great hearth burned steadily and wood laid newly upon it cracked and settled. I heard laughter and raised voices that I knew must come from the dining room, one of them most certainly that of Aegisthus. Music played but I could see no one. The anteroom through which I had to pass was also empty but there I froze for over at the main entrance stood two palace guards engaged in lively conversation. I should have expected their presence, of course I should, but getting as far as this had been my main concern. I waited part concealed by a column and not sure what next to do. But right then there was only one thing I could do. I stepped across the annex to pass by them. They stared at me and one asked, "Where might you be goin' this time of the night an' on yer own?"

I slowed for a moment then, "How dare you question me!" I snapped from beneath the cowl and pulling the gown tighter about myself I carried on walking at a deliberately relaxed pace although I wanted only to run. My spine tingled, I felt their eyes were hard upon me, I almost felt a hand on my shoulder, but I told myself they had no reason to detain me for they surely could not know who I was. Before me the stone ramp sloped away from the palace buildings to pass through the west of the city before ending a short way from the Lion Gate. The night was clear, there was a half moon, the stars above a myriad of shining jewels and the cool air a wonderful – yes, an oh, so wonderful breath of freedom. I passed only a group of robed priests and eventually, before reaching the gate, I turned aside to the flight of stone steps that descended to the grave circle. The steps were engulfed in deepest shadow and I trod in fear of tripping. At last I attained level ground and before me lay the dimly lit walled area where stood the gravestones of Atreus, of Agamemnon and other royal worthies. I stared across but could make out no sign of life, no other presence. Close to the centre of the circle arose the stela of Agamemnon's tomb. This I approached and certain now that I was quite alone I sat upon the ground close to it and waited. I tried to relax but I could not. I moved to lean against the stone and became aware of night-time sounds; of chirping insects, the occasional hoot of an owl and further away in the town, an intermittent yapping of dogs. There, too, were raised voices from the taverns but all was lost to the vastness of the night. I began to think over everything that had happened since the amazing stroke of luck that had enabled Chrysothemis to visit me, of those following days of hope and lastly of my escape that night. I actually felt a degree of pity for the guard I had lured then locked away as he slept on my bed; what might his fate be? That, perhaps, would depend upon mine – to which my thoughts now turned.

I gazed up at the stars and prayed the gods might look favourably upon me. Had I counted the days correctly? Was Orestes to arrive this night? What would befall me if he did not? I couldn't flee Mycenae, especially alone. I no longer had anything of real value and except for goblets there wasn't much else of any worth I could have taken from my rooms or from the other two. If Orestes never appeared, where could I go? Argos and Corinth were the nearest towns but I could never find my way in this bleak night or even the following day without help. Argos and Corinth were also allies of Mycenae so news of my arrival might reach mother and her having me returned would plunge my life into a state of misery I would no longer be able to endure. I listened hard for footsteps, for voices, I stared all about but a shroud of despair was already closing about me. Returning to my chamber well before dawn might be my only option as long as I could placate the man I had imprisoned.

Yet still I waited.

There were sounds. Vague sounds but not sounds of the night. I stood and placed a hand upon the cold slab wondering whether I ought to hide behind it or stay where I was. Figures had entered the grave circle, my heart was racing and now I could just distinguish dark forms moving against deeper shadows.

"Electra."

Someone called my name in low voice and I knew that instant who it was. "Orestes!" I answered, louder than I ought to have and as I leaped to my feet I was in tears of joy and thanking mighty Zeus. There were three of them with Orestes and as they approached closer I knew even in the gloom who they were though each wore a dark cowled gown similar to my own; Chrysothemis and Eriphia of course and there, too, was Pylades. They pushed back their cowls, the two men loosening their gowns so I could observe more clearly their pale tunics and the sword each carried at his belt. Orestes, now a grown man with all the bearing and attributes of a warrior, hugged and kissed me warmly. Pylades, the one I had so much admired in my days of freedom, followed suit and I saw there again the true friend of my brother though he was of sterner feature than I remembered with darker hair and a modest beard. Despite the darkness of that night, light and life were all around, the stars above were singing and I was swept by a tide of hope that all but overwhelmed me. I wiped away my tears with the sleeve of my gown as Orestes spoke, "This is wonderful, you've hardly changed, I can tell even here - but how did you manage to get out?"

I explained as much as I needed then asked him in turn, "Can we get away now? Surely we must leave Mycenae before they find I'm gone or somebody recognises us."

"Not yet, no," was Orestes' firm reply, "there are debts to be paid to you as well as to myself and they will be paid by that man Aegisthus."

"What d'you mean?" I asked.

"What I mean is, this kingdom is mine by rights and I intend to secure that claim tonight while no one suspects anything – unless that guard you locked away has managed to escape."

"No, I doubt that but Aegisthus has men loyal only to him for protection – five of them, and they may be close by our mother's rooms. Can we not leave here now; can you not raise men in Phocis or better still in Sparta?"

"I ran away once," he replied, a hand falling to his sword hilt, "but I'll not do so a second time."

"I will be with you," declared Pylades, "and no one will stand in our way."

"So there we are," grinned Orestes. "Now I imagine the happy couple will have taken to their bed but as I left several years ago my recollection as to exactly where that may be is rather vague. Are you able to describe where we'd find them?"

I thought hard before answering. I was loath to return to the palace but I had to support my brother. "Easier if I show you the way," I said.

160

"And I'll join you," put in Eriphia. "It will make more sense if the guards think we've been out to enjoy ourselves, if you see what I mean."

"Sounds a good idea," added Pylades. "A pity it is we haven't."

"Well you know my feelings about all this," declared Chrysothemis, but you're not leaving me out here on my own."

"Absolutely not," said Orestes.

"And where's Phoebe?" I asked.

"She has less involvement with what's going on than any of us," replied Orestes, "so I insisted she waited in one of the small gardens close to the palace where these other two ought to be. Look, I don't want to delay any longer. Let's go now."

"Yes, now," agreed Pylades, "my sword is itching to do business the same as yours."

We moved across the grave circle and ascended the steps up to the deserted ramp, pulling cowls back over our heads as we went. No one spoke as we approached the palace buildings and the anteroom to the megaron. There were the same two guards, lounging about in conversation as before. On seeing our approach they stood apart with spears crossed ready to challenge us. I saw Orestes and Pylades were ready to slip open their gowns and draw their swords but Eriphia stepped forward and swished back her cowl, saying with a smile as her long hair fell loose, "Please don't spoil our evening; we've been out for a bit of fun, that's all, really."

"Yes, that's all," I added, joining her. "You let me through earlier this evening didn't you but we'd rather avoid a fuss in case our parents get to know about it."

Even with burning torches inside the entrance there was too little light for them to see our faces properly but the guards lifted aside their spears with one of them grinning, "Yeah right, in y'go but best not make 'abit of it. Never know who's out there at night do we."

Eriphia smiled sweetly at each of them as we passed them by. My sigh of relief was, of course, inward.

We proceeded by the megaron where most of the torches were now extinguished, though the fire in the great hearth still smouldered. Further past those steps leading up to my own rooms were the darkened stairs that accessed the royal apartments. I was once more full of apprehension as I indicated these to my brother. I paused for a moment then, "No, I have to go with you," I declared. I was possessed suddenly by a desire to witness revenge. The words I uttered arose from the turmoil within. "After what she and that damnable man have done to me and to others I want to see them suffer."

"Aye, they'll suffer," added Pylades, "though I'd rather you stayed out of this."

Orestes looked as if he was about to insist on my remaining with the others but my expression was more than enough to stay further comment from either of them. He eyed Chrysothemis and Eriphia, saying, "The two of you go and find Phoebe or stay here, quiet and out of sight."

"I'll certainly stay out of sight," muttered Chrysothemis. "I'd rather be miserable and alive than brave and risk being dead."

"I'll keep you company, dear," said Eriphia, squeezing her hand as she kissed her cheek, "then we can be miserable together."

I walked over to the steps with Orestes and Pylades following. "Up here," I said. We made our way to the top in silence but it was more than the climb that had my heart beating hard. Before us opened out a rectangular area where a single torch in its wall bracket threw our shadows as swaying, billowing dark cloud forms about the painted walls. I indicated a passage leading off into obscurity to our left. "I'm guessing Aegisthus' men must now have quarters of some sort along there," I informed Orestes and Pylades, "otherwise they'd surely have guards posted around here. Beyond that door in front of us are the rooms *those* two occupy."

Even as I spoke the door in question opened and a girl appeared, backing out from the room, a slave of theirs I thought, though it hardly mattered. She turned, saw us, lifted hands to her face and was about to dash back into the room when I stepped forward and said, "We mean you no harm." As I spoke I recognised her; it was Melia, the slave girl who years ago had served and kept me company until her visits had been denied. She stared at me in wide-eyed disbelief then Orestes, having no idea just then who she was, pushed by, hand on his sword hilt and said loudly, "Move away and get yourself downstairs!"

"Wait in the megaron," I told her.

163

The poor girl fled to the steps without a word and was gone. At the same time a shrill voice sounded from within the suite, "Who is there? Answer me – who is out there?"

What was I about to witness? Would this be a fight to the death between these two men or would Aegisthus give way and surrender to Orestes? I hoped for the latter, for in spite of my hatred of Aegisthus and my contempt for our mother, I did not care to witness bloodshed. I wanted to have them both utterly humiliated and begging for mercy, perhaps flogged, yes, even my own mother - flogged then driven out of Mycenae forever.

Orestes strode forward to enter the main room with myself, devoid now of all caution, following close, while Pylades remained by the door. This was, after all, a family affair. The sparingly lit room was as I remembered it from years before; richly frescoed and well furnished. We passed through to the next room in which, by the far wall, stood a luxuriously appointed bed that faced the door. This room was adequately lit with numerous oil lamps positioned on a table to one side of the bed where also stood the large bronze mirror. Mother, in her white gown, hovered between the lamps and the bed, gazing at us open-mouthed with hands pressed hard to her cheeks. The bed's occupant, staring in alarm, pushed himself frantically upright to reach for a gilded scabbard that lay against the wall to his right. Our mother rushed by but glimpsing Pylades at the outer door she made no attempt to flee the bedroom but instead halted at the doorway where she screamed loudly for help.

"Well, my friend," declared Orestes, drawing his sword as Aegisthus, jerking aside the woollen cover, struggled naked from the bed, "what a pleasant surprise this is – but not so pleasant for you I think." He stepped towards Aegisthus who in those frantic moments had wrenched free his own sword and was lunging forward with it raised to strike. To further shrieking from our mother Orestes sprang aside to dodge the blow, deflected the other man's blade, plunged his own deep into Aegisthus' body, then wrenched it free. Aegisthus, his sword rattling to the floor, reeled back and collapsed onto the bed with a high-pitched cry, hands clutched to where blood issued freely from between his fingers as he writhed from side to side. Orestes' agility and the speed at which he moved meant that the likes of Aegisthus could stand little chance against him. My brother calmly wiped clean his blade on the bedding while Aegisthus continued to squirm, choking and gasping away what remained of his life. Orestes stared hard at our mother who stood in shocked silence with her hands raised. He levelled his sword at her and asked, "So now - what do *you* have to say for yourself?"

I, too, should have been shocked at what I'd just witnessed but just then I felt strangely calm. I was living a dream, a lurid dream, until her voice rang through the room. "Electra, tell him to keep away from me! I'm your mother – I'm mother to you both am I not!"

"Mother?" I cried, pointing a finger of accusation at her. "How dare you use the word! You would have seen Orestes murdered and cared nothing of it; we both know that don't we! And just look at all the years you've cost me! Yes, listening to you now, I really wish you were dead as well as that – that vile creature of yours laying there on the bed!"

We heard men's voices from beyond the outer room. Someone shouting. Orestes turned and was heading for the door when I cried out to him, "Orestes, watch her!"

Our loving mother had stooped to seize Aegisthus' sword and, clutching it level in both hands rushed forward to strike Orestes in the back. He spun about as she was on the point of doing so, struck the sword from her hands, drew back his own blade and thrust it deep into her side. She gaped at him, lips moving as if to ask, "How could you do this to me?" but even as he withdrew the blade, even as she fell to the floor gasping away her life there sounded more shouting and an echoing clash of bronze upon bronze from where Pylades had been waiting. Orestes strode to the bedroom door to see Pylades, his back against the wall outside the main room, fending off three of Aegisthus' men who had responded to the call for help and the commotion from the royal chambers. My brother strode forward to his aid, all but severing the sword arm of one man as he was poised to strike Pylades, then running him through. I watched as a second man, distracted by the sudden fate of his companion, fell to a skull-splitting sword blow from Pylades. The remaining assailant, his face already slashed and bleeding profusely, saw death loom large, dropped his weapon, turned and fled to the

166

stairs. No longer a dream this was a world of bloody violence. Quite unthinking, I followed Orestes and Pylades as they stepped back to the bedroom where both wiped clean their swords. On the gore-drenched bed sprawled Aegisthus, now quite still, and in a spreading pool of her own blood lay our mother, her dead eyes staring wide. The three of us stood as if not knowing what next to do then Orestes said in a low voice, "I did not intend to kill her – no I did not. To slay one's own kin is the most heinous crime in the sight of gods and men."

"You had no choice - no, you had none at all," I assured him. "Do the gods not lay an obligation on sons to avenge their fathers? Is it not the command of Apollo to shed blood for the blood that has been shed?" Those last words I felt were spoken for me by someone unknown.

"You seem well versed in matters of the immortals," commented Pylades, dryly as he slipped a reassuring arm about my shoulder.

"I've had more than enough time these last few years to think about all that," I replied, much comforted by his touch.

"So, what's next?" he asked.

"I will assert my authority as promised," answered Orestes, "but right now I must find the male slaves who attended these two. I will have them wrap up the bodies, clean the place well and sort everything into whatever order they can before sunrise. It is then I intend to take the throne and proclaim myself the rightful king of Mycenae."

167

"I'll be there to defend your right," Pylades assured him, "though I doubt anyone will rise to challenge it."

"I also must be with you," I added.

We glanced one last time about the now silent bedroom and at the corpses of those who had ruled over our city and murdered others for their own satisfaction. I could find within myself not a grain of pity. Outside the door lay the bodies of the two who had fatally answered mother's call. Of Aegisthus' two other men and the one who had escaped injured there was no sign. But thinking of them reminded me of something else. "We must return to my own rooms," I said. "At once, please."

Greatly puzzled at first but in too much of a hurry to ask why, Orestes and Pylades followed me down one flight of stairs, along the darkened passage where startled Chrysothemis and Eriphia watched us pass by, then up another flight, during which time I hinted briefly at my purpose. "The man I imprisoned up here, remember?" We reached the door to find the bolts still in place so these I had Orestes push back so we could enter. The few oil lamps I had left burning still gave adequate light but there was no sign of the guard I had imprisoned. We entered my bedroom to find him snoring loudly but after some vigorous shaking by Orestes he stirred and opened his eyes. Need I tell you how utterly confused the man was? Not recalling where he was or why, or knowing what to say, he was pulled roughly to his feet, allowed to tug on his boots, ordered to leave the room, to re-join his men or to go instead to his home and to say nothing.

"We still have to organise disposal of those bodies," Orestes said to me when the man was gone. "But you now must rest until morning."

"No," I insisted, "there's yet something else I have to do." I followed them down and there we parted. Orestes and Pylades were to re-join Chrysothemis and Eriphia then recover poor Phoebe from her abandoned loneliness. I headed for the great hall where in the gloom I found Melia seated on the edge of the circular hearth. "Stand up and look at me," I said, taking her by the arm. "Are you alright?"

"Yes, I – I think so," she replied, shaking despite residual heat from the hearth. "What has happened?"

"Did my mother and Aegisthus threaten or abuse you?" I asked. "You can be honest with me because both of them are dead. That's what has happened, and no one is going to hurt you – no, not anymore."

"Dead," she repeated, softly, then she looked up at me, saying, "I – I wanted to continue my duties with you but Lady Clytemnestra forbade it. She said if I disobeyed I would be flogged and given to Aegisthus and those men of his to use as they liked. I think I would have died. Please forgive me but I was so afraid all those years ago that I could do only as I was told."

"Melia, you have no need of my forgiveness. Yes, I know we're both a few years older but what does that matter. I want you to be with me again but as my companion, but you'll do so only if you wish because Orestes from this day is to be our true king

169

and I will grant you your freedom." Poor Melia fell tearful into my arms. I had witnessed slaughter; now was a time for compassion.

I lay awake much of that night as images passed before my eyes and sounds of violence echoed within my head. What had happened that day, what I had taken upon myself to witness, would live with me forever. I recalled our childhood days – days when Orestes would run about shouting and waving his toy sword, when he rolled his miniature chariot around in some imaginary conflict, often with Pylades, as both challenged some make-believe enemy.

Pylades – yes, I was becoming more than just fond of him.

Both those men now were seasoned warriors but I hoped my brother, once on the throne of Mycenae, was not to become another like our father, another Agamemnon.

Chapter 7
Curse of The Furies

The next few days would witness Orestes establishing himself in Mycenae. As we expected there was no hint of dissent or opposition to his taking the throne, rather one of an openly welcoming acceptance. Pylades he appointed head of our palace guard, a position his good friend took with enthusiasm, as did the men in turn accept him. Gossip soon spread throughout the palace and the city over the fate of our mother and Aegisthus. It was soon made known, however, that the one time Queen of Mycenae, though never much loved by her people, was to be buried by order of Orestes within the main grave circle close to the husband she had conspired to murder. Orestes decision was based upon a desire to maintain tradition and to raise a degree of respect throughout the Peloponnese for the House of Atreus that it so badly needed. The body of Aegisthus had earlier been taken away in secret to be burned at night outside the city wall.

Surrounded by land-owning nobles, priests, elders and scribes during the days that followed, Orestes consolidated his status in Mycenae and confirmed it further abroad, sending envoys to local cities such as Corinth and Argos then further afield to Sparta, Pylos, Megara, Athens and, of course, Delphi. Envoys would cross the lands back and forth, gifts would be exchanged, new alliances established and old ones strengthened. An envoy was sent also to the King of Phocis, explaining how Orestes had been obliged to recover his own kingdom at Mycenae but wished to maintain a strong alliance with Phocis.

I sat in full court dress close by Orestes as he once had sat by our mother as consort before being obliged to quit the city. My bold and dignified brother, not one for ostentation, wore a lightly embellished tunic but the precious sword at his side was enough to speak for him. As for Aegisthus' three remaining men; Pylades and some of his men set out to round up and have them executed only to find they had fled the city.

Orestes showed but passing interest in Eriphia and Phoebe despite their overtly seductive glances when in his presence. I put this down to his being much taken with the business of kingship but over the following days, being so close to him much of the time, I felt he was becoming distracted and preoccupied with something other than his duties and commitments. I was soon to learn how matters of a more sinister nature were beginning to affect him. Eriphia and Phoebe also vied, not always discreetly, for the attention of Pylades but it was soon to emerge who really occupied his thoughts and to that I will later return. Chrysothemis, after what she had experienced at Mycenae, decided Corinth was after all preferable as her home town. Eriphia and Phoebe decided to return with her.

It was but a day after Chrysothemis and her friends had left Mycenae for Corinth with traders and an armed party that I felt the need to express the concern I felt for my brother. The sun was long since departed from the land and all business in the great hall done with when I left the megaron, where Orestes remained, and went up to my rooms. There I swapped my court dress for a modest plain gown then I returned to find my brother seated by the great hearth in pensive silence. I sat close by him but he seemed at first reluctant to talk.

"Orestes," I said, "you seem troubled – deeply so. Eriphia and Phoebe each had an eye for you but you appeared not to notice. Hm, very unlike you I thought. What is it so distracts you? Surely we have no problems here in Mycenae."

He sighed, raised his head, locked fingers slowly together at his chin, waited a while, looked aside at me then said, "Electra, I am haunted."

"Haunted?"

"Yes, haunted, or do I mean hunted and - and pursued. It began at night before the three girls left Mycenae. In my dreams I was alone. I wandered in some bare and soulless land surrounded by mountains darker than the darkening sky above them. Behind me there was a sound – a sound like the breathing of some predatory beast, a swishing sound that had me look about thinking some - some unseen creature was about to descend upon me. There was something moving in that darkness; a confusion of shadows that seemed to rise higher as I looked on; shadows that advanced and receded at one and the same time – that's the only way I can describe them. As I awoke they withdrew, yet for a short while after I was still aware of the sounds. Now in the light of day, here in the megaron, in the

173

courtyard or outside the palace I begin to see from the corner of my eye, even in brightest daylight where I thought to find refuge, those shadows emerging to follow me. Yes, and I hear them whispering. I feel one day – one night, they will swirl all about to enclose me. You may know what I speak of."

"The Furies," I breathed. "Yes, I learned about the Furies, among other things, when confined by our mother. They begin to torment you because you killed her, that is so, isn't it, even though this was in defence of your own life, yet they never afflicted her after killing our father."

"Yes, the Furies, even though it *was* in defence of my own life. Electra, I tell you and I know already, if this continues and worsens as I believe it will, it could drive away my reason and I would no longer be able to rule here. I doubt I'd be able to rule my own life."

"Orestes, we must do something. Surely you have committed no wrong. Surely the gods cannot see you punished like this."

"That's what I tell myself! Much against my inclination I have of late consulted our priests. They say I have to go to Athens. There I must consult the goddess herself because, as we're assured, she embodies the spirit of truth and divine wisdom and will assist in judging me for what I have done."

"Then you will be gone from the kingdom you have only just won for yourself – for all of us. Who will hold the throne during your absence?" I need not have asked the question because there could be only one answer.

"Pylades," he replied. "He is much liked and respected by the palace guard for they know him as well as they know me from those earlier days when we trained in arms together. He is trusted also by our elders and our priests."

"And shall I be his consort?" I asked.

Orestes summoned his old smile, one that had for some days past eluded him as he replied, "I'd expect nothing less of you and I know Pylades would be delighted – and not just because you are a daughter of Agamemnon, the man who all the people of Mycenae and well beyond regard as our greatest hero."

That was true enough for our father although for me the sun did not shine so brightly upon the image I held of him. But the fact that our mother was never punished for *her* sin bothered me, so I consulted our priests. There I was assured that the gods would have known her forthcoming fate and so prevented what otherwise might have happened – what in fact *was* happening to Orestes. Did I believe them? I cannot say, but I made no mention to anyone else of my brother's tribulations.

***

Orestes tried hard to ignore them – the ever encroaching shadows and whispers that passed back and forth day and night. He fought off temptation to call out, 'Get away from me! Leave me alone!' but giving voice to his thoughts, he knew, would achieve nothing other than to have people regard him as stricken by insanity.

A spectral hint of brightness defined the eastern horizon when a figure in plain, pale tunic and billowing cloak rode from beneath the Lion Gate into cool morning air. At his side was fixed a finely wrought scabbard in which his lethal sword rested and across the neck of his grey mare was slung a leather satchel. Within the satchel rested small but valuable gifts for Athena's temple, gold to pay his way and a flask of water to refresh him on his journey. He would first travel north-east to pass by Corinth then continue on to Megara.

People seldom travelled alone in open country. Lions were occasionally seen but presented less of a danger than many thought and were themselves hunted for sport and for their pelts. A greater peril by far were those bandits who wandered the land in hope of catching poorly defended travellers unawares in this sometimes wooded countryside. The sun was past its zenith, the sea breeze from the bay of Salamis pleasantly cool and the outlaying farms and groves of Megara would soon be in sight. Megara, where he would remain until the following morning so as to set out fresh for Athens. But though distracted by the persistent affliction laid upon him he became aware of men following. Some way behind and to his left, three horsemen had appeared from among the trees and were urging their mounts toward him. Orestes was determined not to take flight, though not wearing armour he might have easily outpaced them. He guided his horse to a sapling tree, dismounted and there tethered her. 'Here we go,' he muttered, eyeing them keenly. The three slowed as they approached. They were rough men, long-haired and fully bearded, threatening in appearance and manner, their attire hardly better than that of vagabonds. Each wore a sword at his side and dagger at his belt. Orestes' own sword hung concealed beneath his cloak and for a time their approach, to his fleeting relief, drove back the Furies. Several paces away the three came to a halt and one called to the other in rustic accent, 'Well set up fellow 'e looks, don't y'think?'

'Aye, well set up I'd say an' likely 'ave valuables on 'im.' While the third, glowering from beneath bushy eyebrows at Orestes called, 'What's in yer bag then?'

'Oh, this and that,' replied Orestes. 'I don't think you'd find anything of interest.'

'Don't think we'd find anythin' of interest, 'e says,' grinned the first man, slipping from his horse and patting his sword hilt, 'well I'd say we'll decide for ourselves on that so we will.'

As the second man began also to dismount Orestes let fall his cloak. Sunlight glinted on bronze as his sword snake-hissed from its scabbard. The first man, taken by surprise, grasped the hilt of his own weapon but too late as stepping briskly forward Orestes plunged his blade deep through the boiled leather corselet at the man's chest then yanked it free. Letting fall his sword the man staggered back with a shrill cry, lurching into his companion, causing him to stumble hard against his own horse which in turn panicked and thudded back into that of the third man who, cursing aloud, was almost thrown from it. Growling obscenities the second man was already brandishing his sword but Orestes sprang over his fallen victim to confront him,

177

avoiding his wild swing to deliver a deep and fatal blow through the neck. The man spun about, fell, rolled around, choking blood, as the two riderless horses, snorting loudly, pranced nervously about. The third man backed his mount away and Orestes called to him, 'The satchel my friend – d'you still care to take a look?'

Making no reply the man wheeled about and departed in dust-raising haste, not caring to look over his shoulder. Orestes watched him for a time then wiped clean his blade on the clothes of his first assailant. He sheathed the sword, stepped back to his horse and from his satchel withdrew the water flask and drank. There were two corpses and there were two horses without riders, nether horse was of any worth to him, yet in those ensuing moments of calm he wondered what might become of them. Mounting his horse he continued on, once more aware of murmuring and hissing, once more aware of the shadows that were rising up close behind, advancing at both sides; shadows his otherwise lethal blade could never dispel.

He reached Megara and wishing to remain incognito he located an inn where he would spend the night on the straw mattress of a common traveller; a night of torment he expected would be his lot. There, too, was a stable to care for his horse. Orestes did not make himself known to those who were allies of Mycenae and would no doubt have welcomed him. Why – because he could face no one without appearing distracted by that which he would find himself barely able to explain. He drank rough but strong wine, hoping sleep would prevail over the affliction that grew stronger with the advent of darkness. What beleaguered him during the day was once again a nightmare as he attempted sleep. The surge of incoherent voices became a hissing, howling, raging that swirled and swooped about to deny him all but minimal rest. In the morning, with aching head, he took a small meal then, his torment easing a little when the sun peered over the hills, Orestes retrieved his horse and continued on his way to Athens, following the coast around the Gulf of Eleusis before turning inland on his approach to the city. The sun was well into its morning ascent when he passed through the city gate together with traders, farmers and their goods, yelling children and yapping dogs. The noise and life about him proved almost as welcome a distraction as had the bandits. He knew the city from past visits but proceeded on, as in Argos, with no desire to be recognised or to identify himself.

The walls of Athens were impressive to most; even more so the Acropolis that rose above the city where stood the royal palace. But it was not the royal palace that beckoned Orestes. As he approached the temple of Athena to attain his goal he was impressed only by that which oppressed him. It did so as he took his grey mare to a stable close by the temple. The stable-keeper saw before him a man much distracted, a man steeped in anguish, closing his eyes hard even as he spoke. As Orestes approached the temple proper, the satchel containing offerings over his arm, the Furies circled, threatening to engulf him with darkness and mocking whispers, as if determined to deny him

179

entry into the holy place. He stepped up to the entrance, his spine tingling as if touched by an unseen hand, his ears deafened by a malignant hissing. All but unbearable. He stepped forward, eyes once more closed, a hand outstretched to steady himself against a column, thinking to dash his head against it to quell the torment, but as he moved inside the sounds quietened to a sighing breath and the shadows fell away. He groaned aloud with relief, looked about then walked further on into the darkened hall where, at the far end, stood the curtained-off shrine of the goddess. There he stood to wait in silence - an overwhelmingly profound silence unlike any he had known for many days. 'Where is everyone?' he muttered.

A soft voice from behind startled him. 'The Furies may not enter our temple. For a time you will be at peace.'

Orestes turned to face an attractive, fair-featured woman of middle years, dressed in the cowled gown of a priestess. 'I am – I am here to -,' he began.

'I know why you are here and who you are. I have heard much of what happened in Mycenae and I know why the curse of the Furies has fallen upon you.'

'Then you know I have to be rid of them or face total madness,' he told her, not caring to ask how she knew. 'My one respite, my only real respite since this affliction began, was an encounter with bandits on the road to Megara who would have taken my life had I not determined otherwise.

Perhaps that's what the Furies expected and why they held back for a time.'

'Perhaps,' she breathed.

'So what is to be done – what *can* be done? It was Athena our priests advised me to consult and I have with me offerings for her shrine.'

'Athena has spoken already,' the priestess answered, 'and will speak again through me after your gifts are accepted. Place them before her shrine then leave us. The Furies will torment you through the day as decreed but return at sunset and remain with us through the night in peace. In the morning visit our fountain. No one will see you and you will see no one until you are ready. Come to her shrine when you are cleansed and feel at ease. Tomorrow there will be an answer.'

With that she stepped away, pulled aside the curtain behind which lay Athena's altar then vanished down a passageway to its right. Orestes, a little less confused than earlier would leave his gifts, remain a while longer then proceed to any city tavern that offered life, noise and a hoped for measure of distraction.

***

The sun was well past its highest when, in the small, plain room above the temple, Orestes stirred and awoke, shielded from the full light of day by a leather blind suspended across the small window. This was the first undisturbed sleep he had experienced since the Furies had taken hold of him. He arose naked from the bed, glanced at his satchel, scabbard and sword where they rested close by on top of a wooden chest, stepped across and drew

181

away the blind. Sunlight flooded the room and he peered from the window to observe below a small courtyard where the modest fountain sparkled and danced. Seeing the height of the sun and having taken no notice of the room's alignment he at first assumed it was morning. Shortly after, however, he came to realise that he had slept through most of the day and that Helios was not rising but in decline. On a table top next to the window stood a jug of water, a bowl, block of soap and a bronze mirror. Amidst the items in his satchel was a razor so first he would shave the stubble from his face, pull on his tunic then hurry discretely down to bathe in the fountain, assured that, as this must be within the temple precinct, the Furies would not close in to assail him. Immensely grateful to be free of them Orestes accomplished his appointed tasks and in tunic, cloak and sandals he proceeded down to Athena's shrine, for once minus his sword. On leaving his room he had seen no one and thought this very odd. He half expected to find the robed priestess there waiting for him and so she was, but he was surprised to see the main area of Athens' most famous temple as deserted as it had been that previous day. He approached then stood in silence as she addressed him.

'Athena has commanded me to speak with you on her behalf. You were called to stand trial for the killing of your mother, Clytemnestra, and are being judged by those appointed by the gods.'

'Those appointed by the gods?' queried Orestes. 'Who are they? Who are those you say are appointed by the gods?'

'They are as twelve mortals like yourself who in real life would be appointed to sit and pass judgement upon others but here the gods created them, identical in form and in thought. Athena requested for your defence, Apollo, god of light - he who dispels darkness. His priest will join us together with another, unnamed, who speaks for the Furies and will demand your punishment continues. Whatever the outcome a scribe of this temple will later record the verdict.' She closed her eyes, lowered then raised her head to look directly into his eyes then announced, 'Now is the time, for they are waiting.'

'But,' he protested, 'am I not to speak in defence of myself?'

'They know perfectly well what is your defence,' she answered, and Orestes was silent.

From a passage to the right and from another to the left of the shrine, a figure appeared. At the right, an aged, white-gowned man bearing a staff topped by a glittering gemstone, his long fair hair framing a beardless, bright-eyed face that gazed with compassion upon Orestes. This man contrasted altogether with that to the left who wore a dark gown, the cowl of which obscured much of his face in shadow though the gaze of piercing eyes fell with malevolence upon the accused. Orestes remained silent as Athena's priestess turned away from him and stepped forward to face both, saying, 'Have you each presented your case to those who sit in judgement of this man, Orestes of Mycenae?'

'We have,' answered both.

She stepped further toward the shrine, saying, 'Then we will hear their verdict.'

Orestes glanced warily from one man to the other as she entered through the curtains to where the shrine lay. When eventually she emerged she fixed her gaze upon Orestes and said, 'Lady Athena has delivered to me the judgement of those appointed.' Orestes folded his arms, determined not to show the apprehension that so beset him as she continued, 'Six declare you innocent and that the curse of the Furies should be taken from you and six maintain your guilt and say that the curse should not be lifted.'

'In the name of Apollo,' declared the man to Orestes' right, raising his staff, 'I say he must leave here in the light of innocence.'

'And I say he must not!' growled the figure of darkness, gesturing a finger of accusation at Orestes. 'He stands there before us a murderer of his own mother and what greater crime can there be! There can be no excuse. None!'

'The final word in this matter,' declared Athena's priestess, 'has to be that of she who has presided here from the beginning and that decision is now imparted to me.' A tense silence fell before she continued, 'Her verdict is that this man, Orestes, has suffered enough for an act that was forced upon him and so he is therefore absolved of guilt. He must go from here free of further persecution. That is her command.'

'Bah, that won't do at all!' scowled the priest of the Furies as he turned murmuring, 'Can't have it – no, can't have it.' With a dismissive wave of his hand he hurried away and vanished into the gloom of the corridor. The man of Apollo smiled, raised his staff to Orestes then left in silence the way he had entered. Orestes turned to the priestess who informed him, 'There is food and wine waiting in your room. Go there now and think upon what has happened. The curse laid upon you is lifted but remember, though you are cleared of guilt the Furies may not fully accept this and some may linger still.'

Orestes wondered what he should say to her and how he might express his thanks. There were many questions he felt he had to ask but darkness was encroaching throughout the chamber as she spoke again. 'Tomorrow you must leave for Delphi and there consult the priestess of Apollo. Do as she commands, whatever that may be, and thereafter your absolution will be complete.'

She turned away, stepped to her shrine and closed the curtains. Orestes stood a while but there was only the profound silence of earlier. At last he returned to his room where his sword and satchel still lay, taken aback to find three lighted lamps had been placed upon the table. They illuminated a richly decorated bowl of mutton and vegetables, a gilded goblet and an amphora containing honeyed wine. He ate while gazing through the window to a darkened horizon where, high above, stars were beginning to appear. Only voices drifting from the town disturbed oncoming night. The wine welcome; better by far than that on offer at the tavern, so Orestes drank well before laying down on his bed to rest and to think over what had happened. Soon he was asleep.

***

The sun was barely risen when, in the small, plain room above the temple, Orestes stirred and awoke, shielded from the full light of day by the leather blind suspended across the small window. He arose naked from the bed, glanced at his satchel, scabbard and sword where they rested close by on top of a wooden chest, stepped across and drew away the blind. The risen sun, not yet visible from his room, illuminated the city wall, the buildings and temples of Athens and he peered from the window to observe below a small courtyard where the modest fountain sparkled and danced. He hesitated, peered about the room then exclaimed, 'Wait – what's happening here? I feel as though I'm reliving what has already been, but now it's morning, yes, morning instead of evening.' He raised a hand to his cheek to feel smooth flesh. 'Oh, I'm shaved and I feel cleansed. Have I done this in my sleep?'

Again there was food and wine on the table. He stared at these a while then sat to eat and drink, often hesitating, all the time wondering who could have entered the room while he slept? He arose, reached to touch his sword then unlaced the satchel. It contained all that it before had contained, except for those items he had presented to Athena's shrine. 'I – I don't understand any of this,' he muttered. 'The Furies – yes, the Furies must have robbed me of my reason.'

He dressed, fastened on his sword and took up his satchel, then stepping to the door he made his

186

way down to the main hall of the temple. There, instead of silent emptiness, he was confronted by people, acolytes, supplicants, temple officials and scribes, chattering or going about their business. Orestes looked around, not knowing what to expect. A girl in plain dress approached him to ask, 'Are you here to give prayers or gifts to the shrine of Athena?'

'No, I am Orestes, I wish to speak again with your high priestess – is she here?'

'Ah, yes, Orestes; she told us you might return but I fear she will see no one today.'

'But I must speak with her because – because something very strange is happening to me.'

'Something very strange?' the girl queried.

'Look, I don't expect you to understand but it seems I'm beginning the same day as yesterday all over again except that - that now it's morning.'

'Yes,' smiled the girl, 'Sometimes, you know, after speaking with her, people dream but the world as you see it now is the world you must accept. You should go on your way.' So saying, she stepped from him to engage in conversation with another man, one of high rank and attired in courtly robes.

'Dream?' he breathed. 'No, it was no dream. No dream at all when I stood there listening to the results of my own trial.'

Orestes made his way from the temple where a short way beyond the entrance he halted, half expecting the Furies to descend upon him as before. But the shadows that had so tormented were no more than a faded shimmering he could ignore with ease. 'So where does that leave me,' he asked himself, stepping further into the square. 'Delphi - I must go now to Delphi.' He stood looking across the busy square but here in the light of day the world before him carried no more concern than the chatter of people, the rumble of wagons and smell of passing oxen. Glancing about, wondering if something untoward was to happen, he walked to the stables where his horse was kept. Ready to mount and leave, he asked the stable keeper, 'How many days am I to pay you for?'

'Two days, sir, if you please,' the man replied.

'Two days, you say - not three,' said Orestes, handing the man an appropriate snippet of gold.

'No, sir, just two days, that were all you've 'ad.'

***

At midday the following day, Orestes approached the rugged slopes of Mount Parnassus where lay Delphi. In cooler air, he observed many visitors coming and going. As predicted by Athena's priestess, the Furies still remained but were largely ineffectual. From time to time they loomed briefly to one side or the other, discreetly probing shadows seen from the corner of his eye, flickering as if they might advance but just as quickly dissolving away. A minor distraction.

He recalled from earlier years the holy site where lay the oracle of the Pythian Apollo, established as it was in a wild and rocky glen. The priestesses of Delphi were known as the Pythea. Supplicants came wearing laurel wreathes and fillets of wool, and were expected to make sacrifice in order to gain admission to the high priestess herself; one of three, each of which was referred to as the Pythoness when on duty. Having stabled his horse and assured himself of accommodation further down the valley, some way from the temple, Orestes carried on to find a priest through whom he might secure an interview with the Pythoness. The answer was not to his liking; he would be obliged to wait for three days at his chosen tavern.

Impatience was Orestes' lot for much of the time as he made conversation with other supplicants and pilgrims, some of whom related their own encounters with the Pythoness. Otherwise he wandered the woodlands beneath Mount Parnassus, satchel as always slung over his shoulder, sword as always at his side but hidden by his cloak. On the morning of the third day he arose, bathed and set out to purchase from a dealer the creature he would be obliged to sacrifice before the temple in order to gain admittance. A goose. Pointless, Orestes thought, though such acts must provide food for the priesthood rather than for the gods.

After this brief but bloody business, witnessed by a priest of Apollo, he was conducted to the temple by another gowned priest, an aged, long-bearded man in direct service to the Pythoness. This holy of holies he had never before entered and before doing so the priest said, 'You must keep a respectful distance and speak only after I have spoken.' They stepped through the stone portal to descend a short way by steps into a lower level where only modest daylight filtered down. Orestes found the air within unexpectedly warmer than that outside. Both men halted and there before Orestes

189

was the Pythoness. With eyes becoming accustomed to the semi-darkness of this eerie, this holiest of places, he appraised her as the old priest announced in tones that reverberated within the chamber, 'The man I bring before you is Orestes, Lord of Mycenae, sent here by those who serve Athena. He is here to beg total absolution. He would be altogether free from the curse of the Furies who still pursue him though in lesser form. Let me, when he has spoken, gather your words and impart them to him.'

This was one of only a few women Orestes had seen since his arrival at Delphi and her image surprised him in spite of earlier descriptions. Sitting upon a cushioned bronze tripod, she was young and fair, her slim form draped with a fine, diaphanous gown, her head part covered and her right shoulder draped with a shawl of similar material.

The priest gestured for Orestes to speak. 'I am accused of killing my mother,' he announced, 'yet I did so only in defence of my own life after she herself had murdered my father who I ought anyway to have avenged. I have since abandoned my own kingdom through the curse inflicted upon me.'

The Pythoness remained still, her gaze concentrated upon a bowl that rested in her left hand while in her right she held a sprig of laurel from the tree sacred to Apollo. Orestes observed, beneath the tripod, a narrow crack running across the ground. From this arose tenuous wisps of pale vapour that carried a hint of sweet perfume and in the otherwise silent chamber running water could be heard faintly from within the fissure. The girl continued to peer into the bowl as though entranced but now her lips were moving. Orestes had been told by others how the vapour was said to affect the Pythoness, to enhance her powers of prediction and stimulate her prophetic utterances. They said, too, that the bowl contained sacred water collected from that which on occasion welled up from beneath the ground where the tripod stood.

She began to speak; sometimes softly, sometimes in a chanting voice, and now her eyes were closed. The priest, his head tilted back, was mouthing in unison with her, his eyes also closed. She rocked gently on the tripod, her head nodding from side to side, her voice rising. After a while she stopped, leaning forward as if the pronouncement, obscure and all but impossible to understand by her visitor, had been of some effort. Moments later she was again still and poised in other-worldly contemplation.

'The Pythoness has spoken,' said the priest. 'We now must leave and I will say more outside.'

Puzzled as ever he had been these last few days, Orestes followed the priest up into fresh air and bright daylight where they stood face to face. 'Well, my friend,' said Orestes, 'I could make out only the odd word uttered by the lady so I hope her pronouncement meant far more to you than it has to me.'

'Indeed it has,' he replied. 'You must go to Tauris. You must make your way to the temple of Artemis and seize from it the wooden image of the

191

goddess. You must then restore it to Athens where it belongs.'

'What!' exclaimed Orestes. 'This is madness! Tauris is – is -.'

'It is, young sir, at the far end of the Euxine Sea and -.'

'And that's a very long way from here!'

'Ten, perhaps many more days away, as I was about to say, though I myself have never been there.'

'But,' insisted Orestes, 'why have me do that when I need above all else to return to Mycenae? Surely this damned statue or whatever it is can be no concern of mine.'

'The gods work often in mysterious ways,' said the priest. 'They have their reasons I tell you, and I'm assured all will become clear when you have made the journey though she did not say how or why. Meanwhile I'm told that the Furies are altogether banished through your visit here and will trouble you no longer.'

'Well there's something,' shrugged Orestes. 'I'll think tonight about this journey your lady of truth proposes I make. Maybe I'll do it and maybe I won't.'

'You must do this,' said the priest, raising a finger as he turned to go, 'you *must* heed the message of the Pythoness for through her we hear the words of the gods. I can say no more.' With that he strode away.

Angered and confused, Orestes peered about, wondering what best to do. He rested his gaze for a time upon the rising form of Parnassus set against a blue sky, then upon the sacred buildings of Delphi perched in solid array upon sloping ground. He noted once more the varied appearance of the people who passed back and forth; many obviously from foreign lands. He looked along the approaches to Delphi where the land levelled off, raised a hand to shade his eyes. He stared hard. One of the figures approaching had caught his attention; a figure oddly familiar in spite of the distance. Harder still he stared. 'It can't be,' he muttered. 'Not here – no, it cannot be.' He strode forward as the figure, smiling in recognition, drew close. 'Pylades!' Orestes exclaimed, 'what in the name of Zeus are you doing here!'

Pylades stepped up and with one hand resting on his sword hilt he placed the other firmly on Orestes' shoulder, saying, 'I'm here by strict order of your sister. I went to Athens and at Athena's temple they told me I might find you at Delphi and now I have.'

Orestes in turn grasped Pylades' shoulder, saying, 'Well, my good friend, it cheers me greatly to see you but – but why follow me all the way here? And what is happening at Mycenae – is trouble brewing there?'

'There are no troubles to speak of at Mycenae so Electra insisted I set out to find you and offer my support as we've had no news and you've been away for so long. Your sister is confident of her situation but she was most concerned over you, not least because of the Furies.'

'The Furies are gone but it isn't going to help when I tell you I have a long journey ahead of me if

I'm to obey the Pythoness. I did intend to head back home until they revealed to me her message.'

'Oh, so you've consulted the good lady already have you? So tell me, what is this long journey all about?'

'Consulted her - yes I have and this is my third day at Delphi! It was to be my last and had I been allowed into her presence sooner your journey might have been wasted since I'd no longer have been around. Look, I dare say you're hungry and I certainly am. I've spent more than enough time here to find the better taverns so let's get ourselves a drop of wine and something to eat before I find you're a figment of my imagination. You can give me your news then you can have all of mine.'

'I don't have a great deal to report,' said Pylades as they walked away from the temple buildings, 'but the tavern sounds a splendid idea.'

They sat beneath an awning to shelter from the late morning sun and Pylades listened to what Orestes had to say. 'When you get back to Mycenae,' he continued, 'you can tell Electra I have to go to the temple of Artemis at Tauris and lay my hands on some wooden statue they have there. I have to find my way out with the thing before anyone discovers it's gone then I must deliver it to Athena's temple at Athens before I return to Mycenae. I had some trouble with bandits on my way to Athens, two out of three I accounted for, but you'd better not mention that or Electra will worry even more.'

'And why d'you in particular have to steal this statue?' asked Pylades.

'The lady perched on her tripod didn't say exactly why but I believe Athena herself is making use of me and that's something I ought not to dismiss after what I experienced. You'll need to get back and explain all of this as best you can but at least your turning up here and the news you brought gives me confidence to go ahead and make the journey.'

Pylades considered Orestes' words then said, 'Get back – er no, Electra will not be happy with me unless I stay with you. In fact she insisted, so that is what I intend doing. She'd never forgive me if anything happened to you and she made that quite clear before I left. In fact – in fact she had me swear an oath at the shrine of Zeus to do as she asked, so -.'

Glancing up at the sky for some moments, Orestes seemed about to protest, but looked Pylades in the eye and said, 'Very well, so let's get it over and done with. I trust you brought with you a decent horse as we have to ride to the coast.'

'Of course I did. I have a perfectly good horse stabled a short way from here – probably close to yours. I have my sword and I have gold pieces enough of my own so I'll not cost you a fig.'

'Very well,' Orestes said, raising his goblet, 'then there must be people here from Mycenae, though no one has recognised me as far as I know. We'll find someone, a trader, a supplicant, a priest perhaps; someone we think trustworthy who will impart our intentions to my sister and to her alone.'

'An excellent idea,' agreed Pylades, downing his wine. 'Then I take it we can leave at first light tomorrow.'

'Yes, at first light tomorrow.'

Chapter 8
The Priestess of Artemis

I was much concerned about Orestes. He was always headstrong and ready to face a challenge whereas Pylades, though just as brave and as capable, would not look for trouble. I hoped his finding my brother would not prove difficult and that they would return together without undue delay. Before leaving Mycenae, Pylades had asked me if I would marry him. I had always admired this man, even in those days of youth before freedom was denied me. But since he had taken up residence in the palace, since I had come to know him so much better, my feelings toward him had grown far beyond mere admiration and so I had most gladly accepted. We agreed that no mention of this would be made to Orestes until both men were back here so that I could be the one to break the news. I was most disappointed when the messenger arrived from Delphi to tell me Orestes and Pylades were not returning to Mycenae as I had expected but were headed for distant Tauris. I became resigned to this and prepared to wait. Waiting was something I had long ago learned to do.

There were at the time no signs of hostility or conflict in the Peloponnese and there were many duties to keep me occupied. There were also my friends and, of course, Melia. She had so far accepted no offers of marriage though as she was now properly a member of our court there had been a number of suitors. We spoke of this and on one occasion she said to me, "If I marry one of those men I will have to go away and I do not want to do that."

"But why?" I asked. "We're not getting any younger, are we."

"That may be true," she replied, "but you have always been so good to me and I have no wish to desert you unless you or Lord Orestes or Lord Pylades tells me that I should."

I was deeply touched, of course, and I had no desire to lose one whose intimate friendship I had so highly valued over those earlier years as well as since regaining my freedom. "Melia," I said, squeezing her hand, "You will remain my dearest and very closest friend for as long you wish, and neither of those men will have a say in the matter." No, I was sure they wouldn't and there's no point in anyone asking why.

However there was more news to come and it was far less welcome than the first. I was seated on the throne as had been my mother, but without the support of a man, even the likes of Aegisthus, to enhance my authority. I was in the eyes of many a mere woman, whose presence as ruler would be frowned upon throughout all the kingdoms of Greece. Still, the palace guard who so highly regarded and supported my brother also offered that same commitment to me.

But this second news I spoke of arrived twelve days after the first, during one afternoon when I and a small number of my companions, contented with our wine, were being entertained by our newly appointed lyre player and singer of heroic deeds. Two guards appeared, escorting, almost dragging between them a long-bearded man, badly bruised about the face, one arm clutching the other. His attire, though somewhat dishevelled, was that of a noble. As they conducted him around the great hearth to stand before me one of the guards said, "Lady Electra, this fellow will not reveal to us his purpose but insists he brings news of great importance to yourself. He carries no weapon."

The newcomer appeared to be in pain. He stared at me wild-eyed, his lips quivering and I dreaded the thought that he might carry bad news of Orestes and Pylades. I had my companions stand aside, the lyre player to cease, and told the guards, "Release your hold on the man and let him speak."

"Lady Electra," he began, hoarsely, "My name is Lycus, and I am, or I was, a palace noble of Elis – yes, a noble and not one in service. I have fled the city so as to preserve my life because of what has happened there and I beg you, Lady Electra, I beg you to hear me."

"Yes, I'm waiting."

"Our throne has been seized by one Aletes and his close supporters. Aletes is a bastard son of Thyestes, that noble of Elis who years ago fled our city in disgrace with his true sons and came here to Mycenae in the days of Lord Atreus."

"And what has brought you here to tell me this?" I asked.

"He is informed that you now occupy the throne of Mycenae because Orestes has gone abroad and may never return. Hearing this and believing it

199

to be true he sees an opportunity for revenge over what happened all those years ago to a father who it seems had little time for him. He is a reckless man, seeking fame but driven also by drink and an obsession with women who he uses as dogs use other dogs. My own daughter fell to his lusts despite her tender years and I dared voice no objection. I and others advised Aletes against doing what he plans, not least because Mycenae can call upon more armed men than Elis and we saw no reason why your brother should not return, but he dismissed our council. He says the people of Mycenae would rather have a man on the throne than yourself and therefore would offer but token resistance. He will send envoys who he hopes will persuade you to step aside in his favour. Should they fail to do this he speaks of leading a small party into Mycenae during sunset. They will be disguised as a peaceful delegation. They will gain entrance to the palace; they will seize the throne then call in more armed men to enforce their authority."

"But I still await your reason for imparting this news to me when you are or, as you say, were, in the service of Elis and whoever rules there."

"Forgive me, Lady Electra, I will explain further. Our continuing objections, in particular mine and that of a fellow courtier, much displeased Aletes. Two of his men later set upon me with great violence, doubtless with his encouragement, and left thinking I was dead. The other man who supported me was more outspoken and was found that same night outside the city gate with his head severed from his body. To preserve my own life I escaped Elis in an empty hay cart leaving the city at dawn. I tell you - Aletes sees opportunity in mere rumour. His sword arm rules his thoughts. He will bring disaster upon any who follow him – this I know, but he could also be a danger to you. In warning you I hope also to avenge myself upon him and that's the truth of it. I hope also to be of service here in Mycenae."

With further conversation ended I had the guards take Lycus to a place where he could bathe and rest. I ordered clean clothes, food and wine sent to him though he would not be allowed to leave Mycenae even should he wish to. My own companions, until now silent, were most concerned over this man's news and asked what I might do but I was in no mood to answer their questions just then. I dismissed all of them, waited a while then retired to one of our small gardens. The night was young, pleasantly warm and offered me a modest degree of comfort as I sat to consider what I had heard. I could have more guards placed to observe those coming into the city but how would they know who among the traders were genuine and who were not – and most men, even some of advanced age, carried either sword or dagger. I could have more guards placed about the palace and in the megaron and that is what I thought best to do even if it might show up my own weakness in the eyes of others. A knife I would retain concealed upon my own person in case I was confronted by anyone intent on harming me. Meanwhile I would the following day send out three men of our own, claiming to be from Corinth, with genuine goods to trade in Elis. They would surely see or hear of any preparations being made against us by this Aletes and report in turn to me. It might be close to a month, perhaps more, before Orestes and Pylades were back in Mycenae. So for the time being I would retire to my rooms, call for wine and for the comforting presence of my dear Melia.

***

Their journey, mainly by sea, had been long and at times arduous when in rough weather but they had otherwise faced no great danger. Joining trading vessels as it suited them, Orestes and Pylades had crossed the Aegean Sea, passing the island of Lemnos before sailing by once proud now almost deserted Troy to enter the Hellespont. Passing through into the Propontis before entering, via an alarmingly rough passage, the Euxine, or as some call it, the Black Sea, their vessel followed the coast around to its north side before reaching the peninsula where lay the town of Tauris. It was confirmed by their fellow travellers that, ruled by a petty king called Thoas, the people of this far away and modest town were Greek speaking, though with an accent that made their words at times difficult to comprehend. As Orestes and Pylades approached the harbour of Tauris that afternoon in a lowering sun, they saw how the town, well defended with a stout wall, rose up steeply behind with what appeared to be a small palace building set above.

'What have you planned next?' asked Pylades as they disembarked with their few possessions.

'What have I planned? Well, a decent tavern if there's one to be had, a good meal and whatever passes for wine here. In the morning we bathe, we shave, or at least I do – shave I mean; we find out when any boat is soon to go back the way we came then we make our way to the temple of Artemis.'

'For the statue you intend to steal,' said Pylades.

'The very one,' grinned Orestes.

'And you think getting away with temple property will be that easy do you?'

'Well as it's Athena wanting it I hope she'll be around to help us. I'll make a small offering at her temple first thing tomorrow; I have a few pieces of silver.'

'Oh, silver have you,' said Pylades, 'she's bound to appreciate silver – there can't be much of it around here.'

The following morning saw them, each in tunic and cloak, Orestes with satchel, enter the modest town square and locate first the temple of Athena, where he made his offering, then that of Artemis, a somewhat grander building as this was dedicated to the chief goddess of Tauris. On entering the gloomy ante-room they were greeted by a gowned, white-haired and stooping priest of considerable age who inquired in the local accent what their business was as they did not appear to him as supplicants.

'We're just passing traders,' replied Orestes and wish to leave gifts of value for the goddess, preferably before her statue, of which we've heard much.'

203

'And where might you be from,' asked the priest, 'not hereabouts I think.'

'From the Peloponnese,' answered Orestes.

'From Mycenae, actually,' added Pylades.

'From Mycenae, is *that* so,' breathed the priest. 'Then I will inform our high priestess of your presence. She will be most interested, of that I'm certain.'

As he walked away to enter the temple proper, Orestes said, 'You know, my friend, I have a feeling you ought not to have mentioned Mycenae; did you see the look on his face?'

'I know what you mean,' muttered Pylades, 'but I can't think why.'

The old priest left the ante-room, entered and crossed the main area, passed from this and entered a private, colourfully frescoed chamber where, discussing matters with two elders and her scribe, sat she who spoke for the goddess all of Tauris held in reverence. 'Excuse my interruption,' he said, offering a bow, 'but we are visited by two strangers from, er - from Mycenae.'

She stared at him and rose up slowly, saying in a grave manner, 'Oh, from Mycenae are they – well go now, quickly, and summon those guards posted closest to the temple and inform them we have intruders here with ill intent. I will go to my seat where supplicants are assessed so we'll expect those two in there as soon as I'm ready.' She left her associates behind to shrug and glance at one another in puzzlement.

'I guess we have to find our own way in,' remarked Orestes after they had waited a while.

Pylades followed as they moved cautiously into the main hall where they observed the veiled and richly gowned priestess of Artemis adjusting herself upon a cushioned seat close to the temple altar. They moved closer but then, hearing sounds behind, they hesitated and looked around.

'We're being followed,' muttered Pylades.

'So we are,' breathed Orestes as six armed men entered the hall at their rear. 'And they don't look too welcoming. Tricky don't you think.'

'Aye, tricky,' repeated Pylades as the stern-faced guards drew closer, each with a hand on his sword hilt.

'Let's see what her ladyship has in mind,' said Orestes as they continued forward to stop before the seated figure. 'I apologise for our intrusion,' announced Orestes, glancing once more at the stern-faced, guards who now all but surrounded them. 'We stand here before you as ordered by the Pythoness at Delphi and we bear gifts for the goddess.' He looked again at the guards who appeared ready to draw their swords and added under his breath, 'She said nothing about our being murdered.'

'Maybe that's the bit you missed,' muttered Pylades.

Several heartbeats passed before the priestess responded, 'I am authorised by our king to make any decision I wish to make within the confines of this temple. You are from the very place where her ruling king, my own father, would have had me slaughtered before all of his army on the advice of his damnable priest had not Artemis herself intervened to save my life! I swore long ago that should I find anyone from that blighted city in this shrine of ours then they would be taken for execution upon my orders. What have you to say before I have you removed from my presence?'

'*Your* father!' exclaimed Orestes as the guards part drew their swords. 'What trickery is this? If you speak of Agamemnon who fought at Troy then that man was *my* father also!'

She arose slowly from her seat, pulled away the veil, stared hard and long with wide, blue eyes then said at last, 'Your father, you say? *Your* father!' A long pause then, 'Oh - yes, I see now! Yes, you are – by the gods I see before me my own brother! Yes, you *are* Orestes and I know the man you are with though I do not recall his name.' She raised a hand to the guards and informed them, 'You may leave us now but stay close outside.'

As the six turned and left, Orestes declared, 'Then you - you must be Iphigenia, the sister who we thought was long dead and, and now I recognise you also. This is – this is quite amazing and really must be the will of the gods!'

Iphigenia stood gazing at both men. Eternal moments passed before she spoke again 'Th-this has shaken me. I should have welcomed you but because your names were not announced it was my intention to have you put to death.'

'Good job the woman knows you,' breathed Pylades.

She stepped down to stand before them, saying, 'Please, you must forgive me; all these years I have been assailed by bitter memories but now, seeing you, my brother and his companion standing here in my temple, it's as if a dark mist of hatred has been swept away and I once more can see clearly. We will go to my chambers; there you can refresh yourselves and I'll call for wine. I'll listen and you must tell me all that has happened in your lives since the day I was taken from Aulis.'

They sat in the privacy of her colourfully decorated room and Orestes asked, 'Do you not meet traders from the Peloponnese? Do you not hear of what goes on throughout Greece? I now rule over Mycenae, or would do so if I were there where I ought to be.'

'And I'm supposed to make sure he gets back in one piece,' added Pylades.

'I – no, I don't hear much at all because I don't trouble to listen,' said Iphigenia. 'I concern myself only with the affairs of this temple and the people of Tauris. This town sees men who call to our port in their vessels for supplies when trading for grain further north but I never cared to get involved. My world has been the temple of Artemis where I have lived a life of peace, far from the House of Atreus which I know was cursed together with those belonging to it and those who followed. Yes, Tauris is well away from all that. I'm aware Troy was overwhelmed and burned because that is known and spoken of by everyone and some time ago I heard it mentioned that our father is dead. Is that true?'

'Yes, murdered by our own mother,' Orestes replied. 'And I killed her in turn but not through prior intent.'

'It was self-defence,' commented Pylades, 'I saw it all.'

'That is so,' continued Orestes. 'Dead also are her lover, Aegisthus, and that old charlatan, Calchas, who insisted upon your sacrifice. Something he seems not to have predicted was his own death at the hands of an angry petitioner.'

Orestes continued with more news – news of his persecution by the Furies, his visit to Athens and then to Delphi. Goblets were filled and Iphigenia said, 'There is little beyond my duties here that has been of concern to me but news from far to our east has reached Tauris over the years and there have been increasing numbers coming to make sacrifice at this temple through fear of their safety.'

'And what news would that be?' asked Pylades.

'News of tribes on the move, of lands ravished by barbarians who take and destroy villages, settle for a while then move ever westward. It seems the east is a source of many evils.'

'And those evils move in this direction,' said Orestes.

'In this direction so it's said but the truth of it lays hidden within mists of rumour and so is difficult to resolve. Our king appears far from concerned and sometimes I feel Tauris is a town slowly dying.'

'Does this man Thoas treat you well?' asked Orestes.

'He lets me get on with my life and my responsibilities so – yes, in that respect he treats me well, or should I say he ignores most of what happens here and much else outside for that matter.

Wine and women of the court are his main concern, just like the only son who is expected to succeed him. His son has asked me often to give up my position here and marry him but he's of no interest to me.'

'So what happens now?' queried Pylades, glancing aside at Orestes.

'Yes,' said Iphigenia, 'you travelled all the way to Tauris with a purpose in mind did you not. Tell me what that purpose is.'

'Er, yes,' said Orestes, glancing uneasily at Pylades, 'we, or I, came here as instructed and I still have that task to perform on behalf of Athena.'

'You seem reluctant to enlighten me.'

'I - I was told by the Pythoness at Delphi I must take the wooden statue of Artemis from this very temple and return it to Athens on our way back to Mycenae. Athena's priests claim it rightfully belongs to their city. What a difficult decision this has become now we've met you, a high priestess of Artemis who turns out to be my own lost sister alive and well.'

'Aye, a difficult one,' muttered Pylades.

Iphigenia looked from one to the other, drank the remains of her wine then said, 'That statue I understand *was* stolen from Athens many years ago but it plays no great part here. Through this morning I will pray to Artemis for guidance. Return here after midday and join me for food and wine; the guards will not bar your way. Perhaps then there will be an answer. There has to be, has there not.'

They later sat away from the hot sun in a shaded area of the market square and Pylades asked him, 'What if Iphigenia says you can't have the statue – what then?'

'Yes, I've been thinking over that one,' replied Orestes. 'We either leave without it, which I really cannot do, I steal it from under her nose, which I don't want to do, or -.'

'Or what – or need I ask?'

'Right - or you steal it and get away from Tauris, I tell her I didn't know you were going to do it - then I say I'll get after you and recover the thing. That way we're both out of here.'

'You surprise me, Orestes; treating your dear, long lost sister like that. She'll probably call upon Artemis to punish us both – then what?'

'I suppose you're right; got any better ideas?'

'Better ideas,' muttered Pylades. 'No, not really; you consulted the Pythoness – remember? I came along because Electra wanted me to help make sure you didn't get yourself killed.'

'Very well, then I'll have to play the victim in all of this and hope it does the trick.'

The sun was passing its highest and the heat becoming oppressive when they returned to the temple of Artemis. They stepped unchallenged through the anteroom and into the cool of the holy chamber where, before the shrine, sat Iphigenia. Two other priests and a scribe were present but all she dismissed.

'Orestes, Pylades,' she said, softly, 'come close and listen to me.' They approached and stood before her as she informed them, 'Artemis has spoken and wishes her image transferred to Athens.' There were two discrete sighs of relief as she continued, 'It will

210

be safe in Athens but less so here in Tauris. She blesses you both and more; she says that the curse laid upon the House of Atreus is finally lifted. She informs me there is no shrine devoted to her in Mycenae and therefore I must create one there with your help.'

'*You* have to create one?' queried Orestes. 'You mean you'll be returning with us?'

'Yes, I will return with you. It may take a while for Thoas to realise I'm gone, or the statue for that matter – unless he's forgotten it was here in the first place. I will re-join Electra who I so dearly would love to see again after all these years. And Chrysothemis, is she in Mycenae also?'

'No, she lives in Corinth but that's no great distance from Mycenae.'

'So when and how d'you propose we leave?' Pylades asked.

'The way we came, I guess,' answered Orestes. Trading vessels going west must call here often enough and we still have the means to pay for our passage and obtain a horse and cart when necessary. But this statue – I trust it's not too conspicuous or too large to handle.'

'Not at all,' said Iphigenia. 'And as it never belonged here in the first place, it is kept aside from the altar and will be easy to conceal. It must mean a great deal more to Athens than it ever did to Taurus.'

'So, Pylades and I will go to the harbour tonight and negotiate our passage then we can leave at first light.'

'I wonder,' sighed Iphigenia, with tears shining in her eyes, 'who will take my place here after years that have given me peace and happiness away from all the bitterness and troubles of the world beyond. Yet now, Orestes, now you are on the throne of Mycenae perhaps I will shed much of that bitterness and hope to see some of the life I ought all along to have had.'

***

On the eighth morning after hearing the news from Elis I was seated, with a scribe present, discussing a matter of land dispute between two of our court-attired nobles when I observed three robed and cowled figures appear at the far side of the megaron. They moved into shadow between two columns and I wondered if they were present with mischief in mind. I was about to summon the guards when one of the figures momentarily pushed back his cowl, waved his hand, smiled across at me and placed a finger to his lips. You can imagine the sudden, overwhelming relief I felt when I saw who it was. I arose and dismissed those gathered about me. It was obvious that Orestes, apart from not having sent ahead to announce his arrival, preferred to remain incognito. I stepped down to approach them as they revealed themselves fully. The third person I did not recognise until joining them by the hearth but once there I looked at her. I looked at her harder, drew breath then gazed in stark disbelief. Before me stood Iphigenia! It could only be her – the Iphigenia I had for so long assumed dead. At first I could say nothing. I simply glanced from one

212

to the other then again at her, all the time bathed in the radiance of their smiling faces.

"Well we're back at last," announced a broadly grinning Orestes as if he and Pylades had been gone for only a day or so.

"That we are," added Pylades, kissing me with tender warmth.

"And so you are!" I cried, grasping and kissing each in turn. Iphigenia I kissed and hugged especially hard, again and again, saying, "Dear Iphigenia! Oh, I thank the gods! You are a dream come true! You really are, yes, you really are alive and well after all these years. You must have so much to tell me. Really, I just cannot wait!"

"And you to me in turn," she smiled. "Dearest Electra, I've been hearing all about you from these two. How well you look in spite of all I'm told you've been through; it sounded dreadful."

During those moments of elation all other matters were dismissed from my mind. I stood back, hardly knowing what else to say until I asked, "Have you eaten - have you rested today?"

"We've hardly had time for either," Orestes replied. "We joined a trading party from Athens two days ago and made our way straight here. As you see, I wanted us not to be recognised until I'd first spoken with you in case problems had arisen during our absence."

"But the palace guard; surely they must have -."

"No, we avoided the guards. I recalled a much overgrown gap where the wall had shifted slightly after an earthquake. We used it as children; it's hardly wide enough to admit a dog but we just about managed to squeeze through. A man wearing armour could never do it." He raised a finger then added, "Yes, I must remember to have it sealed off."

"Then go straight to our chambers with your heads covered," I said. "Refresh yourselves while I call for food and wine then come back and join me in the audience room. I'll ensure the megaron is kept clear of people so you won't be seen."

I was left to arrange that which I had promised but you will understand how inpatient I was to have the three of them with me again. I waited and watched as wine and cold food were brought in by slaves whose business it was to ask no questions but I'd not waited long before the three were back with me. As we gathered about the table my thoughts returned to the subject of Elis and I was most concerned to reveal all I knew to Orestes. But first I felt I must ask my newly returned and very much alive sister about her life in Tauris and her reaction upon meeting her brother after all those years. We drank and ate as she spoke, asking me in turn more about my own life and how I felt about the time I was a virtual prisoner in the rooms above after the murder of our father. I was determined then to speak about Elis but Pylades raised his hand to me, said, "I think we ought to tell Orestes now, don't you?"

"Er, yes, of course," I answered after some hesitation as Orestes sat looking puzzled. "Pylades and I are to be married."

"I asked Electra to marry me before I left Mycenae to find you,' Pylades said, 'and to my great pleasure she agreed."

"What!" he exclaimed, staring at us both, "And you kept this from me all the time we were out there. Why?"

Pylades looked at me questioningly and said, "I er, I thought it best to wait in case your sister changed her mind while we were gone."

"No I have not changed my mind!" I assured him, "and I hope you, Orestes, and you, sister dear, will approve for I do indeed wish to marry Pylades."

Iphigenia smiled and clapped her hands, Orestes arose and reached across to grasp and shake Pylades' hand. "Do I approve?" he exclaimed. "Yes I do approve! I approve and I approve again! That my sister here should marry my good friend, the best of men, would be my very greatest wish. I will drink to that right now and on the chosen day we'll light up this gloomy old town of ours with the greatest celebrations she ever knew. We'll have singers, dancers and wine served for all throughout the city."

"Orestes!" I blurted out, pushing my goblet aside and half rising from my seat. "Orestes, there is something else - something I can keep from you no longer!" A tide of sobriety descended upon the room as I began to reveal all of what had been imparted to me by Lycus, the disaffected man from Elis. Orestes appeared oddly relaxed as I spoke, Pylades listened carefully while the expression on Iphigenia's face was one of deep concern

"So," said Orestes when I'd finished, "this Aletes must really believe I'm gone for good. What a mistake the man's made."

"Aye, a big mistake there," nodded Pylades.

"But unless we keep our eyes and ears open," said Orestes, "this could be dangerous. We have envoys coming here frequently and those from Elis might well pretend to be from somewhere else."

"Can they not be disarmed before entering the megaron?" I asked, though I already had guessed his answer.

"That would be demeaning for those sent to us in trust by the ruler of another city, especially the likes of Sparta and Corinth. It would imply mistrust of those who would be expected to treat our own envoys with courtesy. No, we'll need to have eyes and ears of our own inside Elis; unassuming people to listen at their inns and in their town square to observe if they are gathering armed men together and if a party is first sent toward Mycenae."

"I sent three of our men to Elis while you were gone," I informed him. "They were to act as traders from Corinth."

"That's good, yes," Orestes responded, "but sending two more simply to watch and wait won't do any harm if things are happening there; I'm sure Pylades here will see to that."

Pylades nodded, "Of course."

"Could it be men from Elis have already entered your palace?" asked Iphigenia.

I felt sorry for her needing to ask that question as the last thing she expected was to find herself back in the House of Atreus with a prospect of violence under discussion. "I believe not," I replied. "Since Orestes left Mycenae, then after him Pylades, all those paying visit to our court have been familiar to me. Also I've had our courtiers, our priests, our slaves and others keep careful watch on all outsiders who have entered the palace, and slaves to watch less frequented areas day and night."

"Should I not start gathering our men?" asked Pylades. "Could we not strike at Elis before they are fully prepared?"

Orestes thought for some moments then replied, "Elis may not be as strongly defended as Mycenae but winter is almost upon us and bad weather could lessen our advantage in numbers if we were obliged to lay siege outside their city wall. I say we should have this rogue Aletes do the hard work instead; I'm sure he'd welcome the opportunity to pay us a visit. Meanwhile, I will for now remain out of sight. Our own people must know nothing of my return until we're good and ready."

"But they'll know I'm back," said Pylades.

"Fine, say nothing or tell anyone who asks that you never found me. If Aletes has spies here in Mycenae it'll be all the better if they hear that. We can make out Iphigenia is your cousin from Corinth – no one will connect her with what happened all those years ago when the fleet was delayed at Aulis." Orestes picked up the amphora, refilled our goblets then as we drank he revealed to us an outline of his intentions.

Later, when alone with my sister, I said, "Don't worry about Aletes; Orestes knows what he's doing."

"I'm sure you're right," Iphigenia replied, but she sounded none too convinced.

"Look," I assured her, "When this is sorted out you should find yourself a man. You're an attractive woman and as a part of our brother's ruling house you'll have no shortage of suitors. Maybe you'll end up in Corinth with Chrysothemis."

"A man," she mused. "Perhaps you're right, though I managed well enough without any of them at Tauris - then being a priestess that's what was expected."

I squeezed her hand, saying, "Let's see, shall we. Let's all play our parts as best we can."

***

The sun had passed its midway point above Mycenae when on the fifth day after my brother's return, when the air was cooler, three robed men, one of them a staff-bearing envoy, arrived and requested to speak with me. I sat in the megaron as reigning queen, attired in long, flounced dress with open-fronted bodice. The fire in our great hearth burned bright and lively, the hall was almost deserted but a scribe stood by my throne with his tablet busily taking my words and our lyre player continued to soothe with his notes. On being informed of the newcomers I dismissed all those in attendance and called for two armed guards to escort the three into the megaron. I ordered the guards to remain standing close by.

That my visitors had declared themselves as being from Elis rather than pretending to be from somewhere else was reassuring as well as something of a surprise. Their openness, I felt, precluded the likelihood of initial deceit or danger. With one holding the staff of his city, another presented and set out their customary gifts with proper decorum, inlaid items of gold and silver for my personal adornment rather than for any of our temples. An act, you may think, intended to win over my trust though I did not care to dismiss the guards. I thanked the envoys and, having summoned a slave to take up the gifts and place them aside, I waited for the first man to announce the purpose of their visit. He did not. Instead he glanced at me, at my two guards, then back to me as if to ask, "Are these armed men necessary?"

Relaxing my initial caution I dismissed the guards then said, "You have ridden from Elis, with whom we have very little trade or communication; what is the reason for your journey here?" Yes, I *was* taking a chance in letting the guards go but this I considered appropriate though I had my dagger concealed in the folds of my long dress. What good that might do against three men who most likely carried swords beneath their robes I cared not to think.

"Lady Electra," began the staff holder, a short-bearded, soft faced man of calm and disarming manner, "we are sent by Lord Aletes, who wishes you well, with the following message. He offers you freedom from the onerous responsibilities you carry in ruling a great city such as this. He says it is no place for a woman and these challenges should be faced only by a man, one used to conflict, one used to countering with arms the threats of others."

Such a conciliatory message I found darkly amusing as I answered, "Yes, a woman I am but you surely must be aware that another woman, Lady Clytemnestra, once sat on this very same throne and ruled for all those years when Agamemnon, her husband, was far away at Troy, and for almost eight years after his death. Do you suggest that I am less able to rule here than was my own mother?"

Hearing my reply the man appeared uneasy, glancing in turn at his two companions before speaking again. "No, madam, we are not suggesting that, nor is our king, but we know Lady Clytemnestra had for a time her consort, one called Aegisthus, whereas her son, so we are given to understand, fled Mycenae long ago to some other place and returned here a while back only to flee again. This situation must be unsettling for your people and Lord Aletes believes strongly that he will be accepted, even welcomed here for that reason alone. I ask that you agree to his proposal and be assured he in turn will wish you to serve as his consort or his wife should you so desire."

It seems Aletes knew little or nothing of Pylades and that he had been somewhat misinformed or was almost as ignorant of affairs at Mycenae as I was of Elis as he went on to ask, "Will you therefore tender your agreement and that of your palace guard as Lord Aletes is ready to set out very soon?"

"And if I choose not to accept his ever so benevolent offer?"

A silence ensued before the envoy spoke again. "Lord Aletes is, I assure you, a man of formidable will and – and is most unlikely to accept your refusal."

"Oh," I responded, "it seems your king's proposal, as you put it, has now become a threat. Am I right?"

"That is not a word I care to use," shrugged the envoy. "I can only pass on what I am told of his intentions."

I of course was already aware of his intentions but had to play my part as a woman alone and vulnerable. I remained silent for as long as I thought appropriate, then, "You are right," I said at last. "I must confess I nowadays find the throne of Mycenae ever more of an imposition and never could I imagine myself able to command men in times of conflict. But I know nothing about this man Aletes – not even of his appearance."

For the first time, the envoy smiled as he replied, "He is a big man, strong as a bear, fierce as a lion and without mercy to those who defy him. He is thought most impressive with his great beard and horned helmet. Another Heracles, perhaps."

Wondering, then, why he'd not been at Troy I made no pretence of being impressed but said, meekly, "It seems I have little choice in this matter. If I give you my agreement, if I inform our own men of my decision, what then?"

221

"Lord Aletes will set out with his armed escort, the best of his warriors that is, and enter Mycenae in peace to declare himself your new king."

I took his words to mean Aletes intended to bring with him a small army. What else could he mean? I was silent yet again before replying, "Then you may tell Aletes that I accept."

"This is wonderful news, Lady Electra" said the envoy, his smile broadening further. "If we ride from Mycenae early tomorrow we will stand before Lord Aletes the morning after with your reply and I'm sure he will set out with his men sooner rather than later."

After further verbal but hollow niceties they left me, guided to allocated quarters by a slave. They crossed the megaron, whispering each to the other, no doubt inflated with pride over what they saw as a successful outcome of their appointed task with no resistance anticipated. Shortly after, I imparted all of our conversation in private to Orestes and Pylades. Not until the day after those three men had left our city, did Orestes reveal his presence to a welcoming court and our palace guard, and over the following days it appeared life would soon return to normal. At the start of this happy interlude I introduced Iphigenia to Melia and both would have much to discuss in what I was certain must become a close friendship. I intended we would establish a shrine to Artemis in Mycenae and Iphigenia would of course be her priestess.

Two days later, during the afternoon, a pair of horsemen, our own men, arrived from Elis and were escorted into the great hall where Orestes was seated in discussion with city elders and various others. I was sat at his side and Pylades was about his duties elsewhere.

The messengers were dishevelled and tired, having ridden all day, but their news was of vital interest. "King Aletes is gathering together his warriors and will depart Elis tomorrow morning."

"How many men will follow him," Orestes asked, "and will they be travelling on horseback?"

"It appears there may be around two hundred," replied one of the men, "but we think as many again will follow them."

"Most will be on foot," added his companion. "Elis does not possess many horses. Their arms will remain in carts drawn by asses until they are close to Mycenae."

"They will of course need to break their journey and rest overnight."

"Aye, My Lord, they will" confirmed the first man.

"I had earlier sent three men acting as traders from Corinth," I informed them. "Did you meet with those men or do you know if they still remain in Elis?"

"My lady," said the first man, "we know of three you possibly speak of only because we heard about and saw what happened to them. They were denounced as impostors by traders from Corinth when they conflicted with businesses these men were trying to establish. Aletes had them seized as spies and tortured but we don't know what, if anything, they revealed to him. They were later impaled upon meat hooks and left to die before all outside the palace. We feared very much for our own lives."

"Then," said Orestes, "Aletes will believe that you, Electra, suspect his intentions. I think it

will make little difference though I'm sure he'll be preparing many others to follow behind his initial two hundred." He turned to Pylades and said, "I trust all our own men will be ready."

"All our men as well as others throughout the city will indeed be ready," he replied, "and I'll have two of our horsemen keep an eye on them as they draw near."

Once more alone I thought hard about the three men condemned by Aletes. I had sent them to excruciating deaths in order to prove my own worth when acting alone. This dreadful man, this same Aletes was soon to arrive at Mycenae, no doubt intending to overawe me.

Chapter 9
The Circle Closes

The morning was fresh, the air cool, the blue sky streaked spectral white when, approaching Mycenae from the west, Aletes, one of the few of his men on horseback, ordered his company to halt. Throughout their journey from Elis there had been no sign of hostility although the ever vigilant Aletes had been aware at times of horsemen watching them from some way to the east with behind them the risen sun. A short distance from the city wall they were aware of people crowded about its top, watching them in silence as his men, talking and laughing among themselves, unloaded their arms and armour from the carts.

When Aletes dismounted, one of his men stepped up to their leader holding forth a horned helmet of intricately worked bronze with cheek guards and swaying red plume. The helmet, when raised and placed upon Aletes head with almost ceremonial dignity, enhanced this tall man's image as a most formidable warrior. Over his goatskin tunic he wore a cuirass of overlapping bronze scales that glinted sunlight, this revealed by the opened cloak of rich, purple wool. It allowed sight also of the finely tooled leather strap, passed over his shoulder to secure at his waist the gem-inlaid silver and gold scabbard that contained his lethal bronze blade, a two-handed weapon larger than that carried by most other men. Aletes was a man attired for conflict as well as for kingship. Another standing close by handed him a ceramic wine flask from which he drank liberally. He handed back the empty flask, spat aside and drew the sleeve of his tunic over his mouth. For a time Aletes stared across at Mycenae, the expression on his face one of determination. An expression soon to become one of grinning contempt.

Sunlight glinted from the bronze corselets, shoulder guards and greaves of those comprising his well selected host, each man a seasoned warrior with sword at his side, each carrying both spear in his right hand with at his left a circular, bronze rimmed, leather faced shield with metal boss at its centre. Fringes or plumes of colourfully dyed feathers of varying length and size complemented helmets of interlocking boars tusks stitched in place over leather caps. Heavy linen kilts were overlain by hanging leather straps, themselves studded along their lengths by small bronze disks. These were men well prepared and eager to engage in combat should resistance be encountered. Concealed amidst the trees some way from the city wall a yet greater number of men were arriving. They would await the sounding of a ram's horn should Aletes wish to summon reinforcements.

The men of Elis assembled behind their king in orderly manner and, having followed the curve of the city wall, they reached the wide path that traversed the valley. Seeing ahead the Lion Gate, Mycenae's great portal, their conversation turned more than earlier it had to what might be gained upon their entry to the city by way of plunder and its women should Aletes allow it. Two drummers, proceeding close behind their king, began to beat out a marching rhythm as they strode toward the gate where the great oak doors were being drawn back by four armed guards until fully opened. Earlier that morning Aletes had ordered two men to ride around the city; their purpose to ascertain the presence of any possible enemy loitering unseen. The two had failed to return but so close appeared to be his goal, with no resistance in evidence, that those men and their task had been all but forgotten. The guards at the entrance had made their way down to the sides of the ramp and out of sight as Aletes, with two men close at each side to counter possible ambush, each with hand resting upon his sword hilt, entered Mycenae with his men following. Having passed beneath the great lintel that supported its burden of heraldic stone lions and emerging now from between the high, inner walls, he raised his hand then called his men to a halt. The drumming also ceased. Aletes considered that for one of his status there ought to have been a formal greeting, a delegation, a recognition of his arrival by rolling drums from ahead, or cheering from the crowds gathered about the rooftops and the city wall, even if such had been pre-ordained. There was none. Members of Mycenae's court should have been at the gate to welcome him. There were none. Aletes and those close by him peered about, listening hard, but an ominous silence prevailed over the city and that section of its formidable wall where people, mainly men, had gathered to watch; a silence broken only by the call of birds wheeling

227

high above. Then a ripple of murmuring from his men.

'D'you expect treachery?' asked one.

'I always expect treachery,' Aletes answered.

But why such silence Aletes asked himself. Did all those people peering across at him not even discuss his arrival with one another? These considerations were dismissed as he gazed along the stone ramp rising ahead where a figure had come into view. There, between himself and the point where the ramp veered to the left stood the woman who he knew must be Electra. Descriptions of her had been difficult to elicit as contacts between Mycenae and Elis had been scarce. He recalled demanding this information from the three Mycenaean spies captured in Elis but, knowing they were to die, they had told him nothing of worth. She stood within easy calling distance from Aletes, her corn-blond hair coiled and clipped in place above her head. A long, colourfully pattered gown of Egyptian cotton emphasised her slim figure. She had chosen not to attire herself formally as a queen or female courtier yet she struck his keen eye at once as utterly desirable and very soon she and her kingdom would be his. Perhaps, thought Aletes, she had felt too ill at ease to bring herself all the way to the gate. Behind her were gathered young men in court dress. Others, ranged further back, were obscured from his vision. With his attention drawn most strongly to the alluring image of Electra, Aletes considered himself at that moment much favoured by the gods – by Mighty Zeus himself. With a cry of, 'On we go, lads!' he gestured with enthusiasm to those at his rear. The drums rattled loudly once more - but the world was about to change.

Not a half of his men had pressed beneath the gate, through the narrow passage and onto the exposed ramp when Electra turned and slipped out of sight between her male companions. Aletes paused, a sudden anger welling within him as he stared at the men ahead to see each loosening and shedding his gown to reveal a gleaming bronze cuirass. Each was now taking up a plumed helmet that had lain concealed behind. Each was transforming himself in those startling moments from onlooker to armed warrior. Spears and small shields were passed to them by those men at the rear who likewise were arming. Aletes, tallest and most fearsome to behold of any man on either side, shed his cloak and exclaimed, 'Oh, we've 'ere a bit of trickery 'ave we!' Seeing how he well outnumbered those gathered to face him on the exposed ramp he muttered, 'Defy me would you,' then laughed aloud, calling his men forward with a cry of, 'At 'em, lads! Cut the buggers down then we take the palace an' its women!'

Seeing at last a challenge to be met the Elians surged confidently on with their drummers beating hard. They unsheathed bright metal blades. They shouted encouragement to one another. All were eager to show their worth in the eyes of their leader when a serpent hiss pierced the air. Those men on the city wall to Aletes right, having taken up their bows, had loosed a storm of flesh-seeking arrows into that side of the Elians unprotected by their shields. A man close to Aletes was among the first to reel back when a lethal arrow pierced the side of his head below his helmet. The drumming stopped, others of his men stricken cried aloud as their companions glanced about in stark confusion. Uproar welled as an angry sea amidst the Elians. Aletes, his corselet having deflected an arrow, discarded his cloak, drew out his great sword, turned to behold what was happening behind him then looked up to see clean-shaven Orestes and bearded Pylades step forward at the head of their own men with spears raised to cast. Their spears were hurled not at Aletes but aimed to pass over his head and strike down those men crowded close to or within the walls of the gateway - those not yet able to employ their own weapons. A second flock of arrows swooped upon them and more men reeled or went down to the rear of Aletes with arms and armour ringing on hard stone. Witnessing the fate of those about them a few turned in panic, clambering over men already fallen or reeling about to stumble from the edge of the ramp. Those outside the gate, unaware of events taking place within, still pressed close, attempting to push through and shouting for those ahead to move on.

On the confined width of the ramp Orestes, Pylades and their twenty or more companions, each with shield in his grip and sword drawn, closed with chilling determination upon Aletes and his forty or so men still willing and able to fight. Moments before they clashed a third swarm of arrows sped down from the city wall, striking into what had become Aletes' hard core of followers, bringing down or wounding several more of their number. Aletes cursed aloud when another of those closest to him was struck through the neck and fell choking blood. Meanwhile those reaching the gate, slipping on bloodied flagstones, scrambled over the dead and injured, shouted, screamed and struggled with shield and sword against their own men crushed within the confines of the walls. From amid this chaos sounded the ram's horn. Reinforcements would be summoned but Mycenae's own armed warriors, alerted by the two horsemen sent out by Orestes, were already pouring in force from the newly unbarred postern to the east of the city.

A look of grim vengeance darkening his bushy-framed face, Aletes stood his ground and bellowed at those but a few paces away, 'Name ye'self whoever y'are an' meet me man to man!'

On hearing their leader's challenge his warriors stood their ground.

Muttering, 'Here I go,' Orestes stepped ahead of his companions to announce, 'I am Orestes, son of Agamemnon and I will defend this city to the death – preferably yours!'

'It's *your* death is what we'll 'ave!' growled Aletes as he strode forward to lunge at Orestes, swearing aloud as with both hands he swung aside his great sword to deliver the blow. His crosswise stroke was intended to decapitate his adversary but his blade was deflected upwards with a resounding crack by the shield of a low-dodging Orestes. Cursing further Aletes raised his sword high, bringing it down with enough force to sever the head from an ox, but ill judged, driven by raw anger rather than by sound judgement, it struck only Orestes' shield, splitting it asunder, but the swing carried his heavy blade down too far. Orestes, having sprung aside as his broken shield clattered to the ground, thrust his sword hard upwards between the metal scales of Aletes' corselet and deep between his ribs. As the blade was wrenched free Aletes staggered aside, turned to peer in wide-eyed, open-mouthed disbelief at Orestes, knowing in his final moments that utter stillness had once more descended all about. With a choking cough Aletes fell, his armour, his mighty sword and splendid horned helmet ringing loud to break the silence.

Tumult resumed with Orestes, Pylades and their comrades falling as eagles upon those of Aletes' men ranged between themselves and the Lion Gate. Pylades, lunged at by a spearman, struck the weapon aside with his shield and dealt its owner a death blow through the neck before turning upon the next man. Amid a clash of metal upon metal, amid shouts and cries, a few of the enemy continued to fight on. More retreated with others struck and falling or leaping in desperation from the ramp to the ground below, there to be despatched by those guards, now reinforced, who had opened the doors of the Lion Gate to allow Aletes' men in. But the gateway was clearing as those outside realised what had happened within the city. Orestes and his men advanced down the ramp, stepping over dead and wounded, emerging to find the enemy outside, stricken by further arrows from above, confused and disorganised. Some offered piecemeal resistance but were soon cut down while others fled to join those

of their fellow men who had been stationed far
beyond the city wall. On hearing the ram's horn
Aletes' reserve warriors had emerged from amidst
the trees and were following around the valley on
their way to the gate. They were closer to the city
wall when Mycenae's archers began to inflict
sufficient injury to stem their advance. Those men
in retreat from the city had now reached them to
give a breathless account of Aletes' death and to
spread the message of carnage and defeat. At the
same time Mycenae's joined up forces, led by
Orestes and Pylades, came into unwelcome view,
ready to engage once more in deadly combat. There
might have been a set battle between two evenly
matched sides but more of the enemy fell to
speeding arrows or well-cast spears while the rest,
knowing their leader to be dead, thought it better to
retreat or to throw down their arms in surrender.

***

On seeing the advance of Aletes I had hurried up to
the city wall where I was able to witness what
happened outside. Iphigenia I had persuaded to
remain by the great hearth with Melia and others of
our friends. I did not want her seeing any of this
whatever the outcome. I was horrified when Orestes
stepped out to face that terrible brute of man alone,
a man large and fierce as any I dared imagine, but
my dear, brave brother proved more than a match
for him. Shortly after that I was able to observe
much of what occurred beyond the city wall. Seeing
this impressed me in other ways for Orestes, as it
turned out, ordered that mercy should be offered to
those willing to give up their arms.

233

Orestes had fought as one possessed by elemental skills, a true son of Agamemnon in his determination to bring down those who challenged him and always with the resolute Pylades close by. Thankfully we had lost few of our own men that day. You will by now have understood what my brother had done; he had lured the reckless Aletes out into our lands, into Mycenae and to his death, using the city itself as a fatal trap.

I did not stay to watch the aftermath, the stripping of arms and armour from the dead or the clearing away of their bodies. Then there was the fate of those wounded but still living. They would be handed over to their own comrades. And what of Aletes? His men asked for his arms and armour but declined to take his body. Orestes would have his remains burned, not outside the city wall but in the market place so all would witness the end of he who dared challenge Mycenae.

I retired with news of our victory to the megaron where I re-joined Iphigenia, Melia and others of my friends. My sister would need much reassurance over her decision to return here after those uneventful years at Taurus. To her it must have seemed the House of Atreus and all its past troubles still afflicted our city. But present troubles or no, better times were soon to be ours.

About my marriage to Pylades, Orestes, I knew, would be true to his word. The ceremony would, as expected, take place in our temple of Hera, wife of mighty Zeus. Mycenae, never regarded as possessing the open and colourful aspect of fabled Knossos was to blossom as a field of flowers on our wedding day. The city would know light and life as never before; wine and good food were to be granted to all, including slaves of the palace and court for this was to be a double celebration. Our citizens would rejoice for Pylades and myself and for the victory over those who had conspired against us.

Elis would fall under the power of Mycenae but having tasted victory, Orestes intended next to turn his attention to the affairs of other towns and cities in the north and west of the Peloponnese. Where there were squabbles or open warfare he would take advantage of the situation, if necessary using force to gain good fortune for Mycenae and her trade and to impose peace. To the south he would further strengthen the alliance between Mycenae and Sparta by marrying Hermione, a daughter of Menelaus and Helen, and herself considered a woman of great beauty. Mycenae would become even more powerful than she had been but would we and our lands be secure for long? Would Mycenae and the world beyond ever truly be at peace? Traders spoke of dark clouds gathering far to our east. Might their storm one day break upon us? But now, for me, in spite of all that had happened, in spite of all those years I had lost and the horrors I had witnessed, the sun had risen anew and my life was beginning afresh.

You and I have been through a journey together. You have seen the best and the worst of our lives in these often turbulent times. As I sit here alone in my retreat to gaze across to the sunlit hills, I hope you will understand.

Credits

My thanks to Matt Poitras at MP Filmcraft, www.mpfilmcraft.com for permission to use his superb Mycenaean warrior images and to Lynda Buxton for her invaluable assistance in reading through and pointing out the numerous textural and other deficiencies in my work.

www.jeffreypeterclarke.com

More books by the author

SHADOW OF THE BEAST
THE MAN WHO SOUGHT ETERNITY
RETURN OF THE HERO
I, MEDEA
THE DEVIL IN EDEN
THE SINGING STONES
HIDDEN WORLDS Volumes 1 and 2

Available from https://fiction4all.com and other good bookstores.